W9-AKX-656

"I need to find a way to convince my mother that she doesn't need to find me a wife," said Michael.

"Is that your business proposition? You want us to act as if we enjoy each other's company when we're with your mother?" asked Cassie, her eyes never leaving his.

"Actually, I think we need to pretend it's a little more than being friendly."

Cassie's heart started to pound faster. Her face felt flushed. "Are you saying you want me to pretend to be your girlfriend?"

"No, I want you to pretend to be my wife."

Dear Reader,

November is an exciting month here at Harlequin American Romance. You'll notice we have a brand-new look—but, of course, you can still count on Harlequin American Romance to bring you four terrific love stories sure to warm your heart.

Back by popular demand, Harlequin American Romance revisits the beloved town of Tyler, Wisconsin, in the RETURN TO TYLER series. Scandals, secrets and romances abound in this small town with fabulous stories written by some of your favorite authors. The always wonderful Jule McBride inaugurates this special four-book series with *Secret Baby Spencer*.

Bestselling author Muriel Jensen reprises her heartwarming WHO'S THE DADDY? series with *Father Fever*. Next, a former wallflower finally gets the attention of her high school crush when he returns to town and her friends give her a makeover and some special advice in *Catching His Eye*, the premiere of Jo Leigh's THE GIRLFRIENDS' GUIDE TO... continuing series. Finally, Harlequin American Romance's theme promotion, HAPPILY WEDDED AFTER, which focuses on marriages of convenience, continues with Pamela Bauer's *The Marriage Portrait*.

Enjoy them all—and don't forget to come back again next month when another installment in the RETURN TO TYLER series from Judy Christenberry is waiting for you.

Wishing you happy reading,

Melissa Jeglinski
Associate Senior Editor
Harlequin American Romance

THE MARRIAGE PORTRAIT

Pamela Bauer

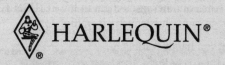

TORONTO • NEW YORK • LONDON
AMSTERDAM • PARIS • SYDNEY • HAMBURG
STOCKHOLM • ATHENS • TOKYO • MILAN • MADRID
PRAGUE • WARSAW • BUDAPEST • AUCKLAND

If you purchased this book without a cover you should be aware
that this book is stolen property. It was reported as "unsold and
destroyed" to the publisher, and neither the author nor the
publisher has received any payment for this "stripped book."

For a woman who has been an inspiration to me
my entire life, my sister Carol Ann.

ISBN 0-373-16852-7

THE MARRIAGE PORTRAIT

Copyright © 2000 by Pamela Muelhbauer.

All rights reserved. Except for use in any review, the reproduction or
utilization of this work in whole or in part in any form by any electronic,
mechanical or other means, now known or hereafter invented, including
xerography, photocopying and recording, or in any information storage
or retrieval system, is forbidden without the written permission of the
publisher, Harlequin Enterprises Limited, 225 Duncan Mill Road,
Don Mills, Ontario, Canada M3B 3K9.

All characters in this book have no existence outside the imagination of
the author and have no relation whatsoever to anyone bearing the same
name or names. They are not even distantly inspired by any individual
known or unknown to the author, and all incidents are pure invention.

This edition published by arrangement with Harlequin Books S.A.

® and TM are trademarks of the publisher. Trademarks indicated with
® are registered in the United States Patent and Trademark Office, the
Canadian Trade Marks Office and in other countries.

Visit us at www.eHarlequin.com

Printed in U.S.A.

ABOUT THE AUTHOR

Pamela Bauer was born and raised in Minnesota where you need a sense of humor if you're going to survive winter. That's why she writes romantic comedies set in the Midwest with heroes who know how to warm a woman's heart...and toes. She has received awards from *Affaire de Coeur* and *Romantic Times Magazine* and her books have appeared on the Waldenbooks romance bestseller list. She currently makes her home in Minnesota where she lives with her husband who is her real-life hero, her two adult children and a bichon-poo who thinks he's human. When she's not writing, she enjoys watching foreign films, going to the theater and fishing.

Books by Pamela Bauer

HARLEQUIN AMERICAN ROMANCE
688—THE PICK-UP MAN
718—MAIL ORDER COWBOY
803—SAVING CHRISTMAS
814—CORPORATE COWBOY
852—THE MARRIAGE PORTRAIT

Don't miss any of our special offers. Write to us at the following address for information on our newest releases.

Harlequin Reader Service
U.S.: 3010 Walden Ave., P.O. Box 1325, Buffalo, NY 14269
Canadian: P.O. Box 609, Fort Erie, Ont. L2A 5X3

Dear Reader,

I love happy endings. Call me an incurable romantic, but when two people fall in love, I want them to have a "happily ever after." The cynics of this world may say there is no such thing, but I know differently. My parents recently celebrated their sixtieth wedding anniversary. Talk about inspiration!

We all know the road to "happily ever after" can be a bumpy one, even for two people in love. Or as my friend Sandy would say, "Marriage is a journey, not a cruise."

It certainly has been a wonderful journey for my husband and me. We've shared joys and sorrows, successes and failures, dreams and disappointments. We started out as two love-struck teenagers, but along the way we became not only lovers, but the best of friends.

In *The Marriage Portrait*, Mac and Cassie's journey doesn't start in the traditional way. They marry not for love, but for convenience. But like us, they get more than they bargained for. I hope you will enjoy their story as they travel their road to "happily ever after."

Warmly,

Pamela Bauer

P.S. I love hearing from readers. You can write to me c/o MFW, PO Box 24107, Minneapolis, MN 55424.

Prologue

"Ladies, it's time for new business," Louella Gibbons, the chairwoman of the Minnetonka Mums, declared with a clap of her gavel. The garden club, composed entirely of senior citizens, had gathered for their monthly meeting. All talk of hybrids and pollination ceased as they looked to their leader.

"I believe Tessie has a request."

All eyes turned in the direction of the white-haired woman who pushed her chair back and stood—all five feet two inches of her. With a somber expression on her face, she said, "I've decided to take you up on your offer to help with Michael."

Murmurs of approval spread around the table, but they were quickly silenced as Louella said, "Order, ladies."

Tessie continued. "I've given him plenty of time to do his thing, but as you know, he's going to be thirty-five next month. I'm afraid if I don't do something, it'll be too late. I'm not getting any younger, either."

"No, none of us are," Agnes Dienhardt contributed.

"And we all know what's happening," Tessie continued.

"The pool's getting shallower with every year that passes," Francine Collona answered with an ominous shake of her head.

"You don't want him to wait so long that it's empty," another Mum piped in.

"He definitely needs a little push in the right direction," Agnes added.

"You all know I'm not the kind of mother to interfere, but…" Tessie trailed off.

"He's leaving you no choice," someone finished for her.

"Exactly," Tessie stated with a knowing nod. "And I have good intentions. I only want him to be happy."

"Of course. We all do. We love him, too," Louella said on behalf of the group.

"Then you'll do it?" Tessie asked, giving the group an encompassing glance.

"Of course, we'll do it, but someone will have to make a motion," Louella answered.

Betty Jean Greer raised her hand and said, "I move that the next project we undertake be the courtship of Dr. Mac."

"I second," another voice said.

"All in favor?" Louella asked.

A chorus of ayes could be heard.

"Anyone opposed?"

Silence.

Louella then decreed, "Passed. The Minnetonka Mums have agreed that they will do whatever they can to assist Tessie in finding Dr. Mac a wife."

Tessie smiled broadly at the group of women gathered. ''Thank you so much. You are the dearest friends a woman could have.''

''That's what Mums are for,'' Agnes reminded her with a pat on Tessie's hand. ''Besides, we've all been itching for you to give us the go-ahead. We have lots of ideas.''

Tessie smiled slyly. ''That's just what I wanted to hear. Should we get down to business, ladies?''

Chapter One

"Good morning, Dr. Mac. And happy birthday." The young woman sitting at the reception desk in the clinic handed him a small stack of pink slips. "Your messages."

"Thank you, Jenny. For both the birthday wish and these," he said, waving the pink slips in the air.

"I put up a sign. I hope you don't mind," she said, nodding toward the waiting area where a computer-generated banner hung on the wall. It read, "Bark for Dr. Mac's birthday."

Dr. Michael McFerrin wished the staff didn't see birthdays as an occasion to celebrate. If it were up to him, he'd treat his as if it were just another day of the week. Get up, go to work and come home. No fuss. No big deal.

Unfortunately, Jenny—and he guessed the other employees at the clinic—thought his birthday merited more than a casual "oh, by the way, happy birthday" wish in passing. He discovered this was true when he stepped into his office and saw the cake. Suddenly, behind him was the entire office staff.

"That looks like an awful lot of fire for one cake,"

he quipped as the tech, Tabitha, began lighting the candles.

"Quick, make a wish," she said, when all thirty-five had been lit.

Mac wasn't one to make wishes. He closed his eyes briefly to humor them, then with a deep breath, blew out the candles. One remained lit. He blew once more, it went out and then burst into flame again.

"All right. So who put the trick candle on the cake?" he asked, surveying the small group gathered around him.

"No wishes for you this year," Tabitha said smartly as she pulled the candles from the frosting. "Who's having cake?"

"I haven't had breakfast," Mac remarked.

"Sir, this *is* breakfast," Tabitha retorted, cutting the cake with a large knife. "I'll cut you a big one."

"First he has to open his present," Jenny reminded everyone.

Present? He squirmed uncomfortably. "Didn't we agree last year that there were going to be no more presents?" He plastered his sternest look on his face.

"You agreed," Tabitha retorted. "We didn't."

Jenny produced a brightly wrapped package. He fumbled with the gold ribbon that refused to come undone. Finally Jenny reached over and clipped it with scissors. "Thanks," he mumbled.

Inside the box was a T-shirt that had a cartoon drawing of a shaggy mutt on the front. Below was a caption that read "In Dog Years I'm Dead."

He grinned. "Very funny, ladies."

"We know you're not dead, sir," Jenny spoke up.

"Well, Jenny does anyway," Tabitha quipped.

"She answers your private line. What's the total so far this month?"

"Only seven. He's slipping," Jenny answered.

"Oh-oh. He *is* getting old, isn't he?" Lynn, the other vet on staff, teased.

Michael didn't need to ask to what the number seven referred. His all-female staff made no secret of the poll they had each month. Instead of having sports pools as most offices had, they had a Dr. Mac pool. Every woman in the office put in five bucks and made a guess as to how many women would bring in a healthy pet just for the chance to spend a few minutes with him.

"Dr. Mac, you should get married and put all those poor women out of their misery," Jenny advised.

He sighed. "At my age, Jenny, all the good ones are gone."

"You're just not looking in the right places," Tabitha told him, handing him a large square of chocolate cake iced with white frosting.

Michael wasn't really looking at all. He'd never had to. Women found him. Ever since he'd played football in high school and college, he hadn't lacked for female companions. And as for marriage, he'd never thought much about it. Why should he? He had a great life as a single guy and he didn't need to complicate it with the kind of love romanticized by songs and movies.

"Are you still dating Julia?" Tabitha wanted to know.

"Oh, good heavens, no. She's gone. It's a Colleen now," Jenny answered.

"It's *nobody* right now," Michael corrected her.

"That might change real soon," Phyllis, the lab tech, said smugly.

"Of course it'll change," another piped up. "It's simply a matter of time."

Michael just grinned in amusement. Over the years he'd grown accustomed to their good-natured teasing.

"Yes, it is. Listen to this," Phyllis commanded everyone, waving the newspaper in midair. "It's Dr. Mac's horoscope for having a birthday today," she announced, then cleared her throat before reading aloud. "'You may help someone who is down on his or her luck by buying his or her wares.'"

"That's nothing new. Dr. Mac does that all the time. He takes Henry's products even though he knows we won't be able to use them all," Jenny reminded everyone.

Phyllis continued. "Your lucky money months are September and January."

"Guess that means we should wait to hit him up for a raise, eh?" Tabitha quipped.

Phyllis smiled, then went on. "'Listen to the advice of a close relative and act upon it.'"

"I don't have any close relatives except Tessie, and I always take her advice," Michael said.

"And so you should. She's a wise woman," Phyllis told him, then finished reading the horoscope. "Now here's the best part. 'Take a romantic risk in the next three weeks because you're more emotionally available to love now than you've ever been in the past.'"

"Oh-oh. Maybe Dr. Mac is finally going to meet his match," Tabitha said with a challenging gleam in her eye.

Michael laughed. "You ladies know I can't give my heart away. It belongs to all of you."

That produced a chorus of groans.

"Spoken like a true bachelor," Lynn quipped.

Michael threw up his hands in defense. "Hey! I'm only thirty-five. Even if that is old in dog years, it's young in man years. And you ladies know I'm perfectly happy being your boss and dedicating my time and energy to what I love most—my patients. Speaking of which, aren't there any here this morning?"

"They can wait," Tabitha assured him. "Finish your cake."

"And tell us your plans for this evening," Jenny added.

"I believe Tessie is cooking a special meal for me. I offered to take her out to dinner, but she insisted on cooking it herself," he answered.

"And so you should let her. She's enjoys fussing over you," Tabitha said. "You're lucky to have such a wonderful woman for a mother."

Michael couldn't argue that one. He was very fortunate indeed to have Tessie McFerrin for a mother. He finished the cake, washed it down with a couple of sips from his bottle of mineral water, then reached for his lab coat.

"Time for work," he announced as he slipped his arms into the sleeves of the white jacket.

"You will keep us posted, won't you, Dr. Mac?" Phyllis asked.

"About what?"

"Whether or not your horoscope is right."

"You mean about the lucky months?" he quipped with a smile.

Phyllis gave him a playful punch on the arm,

prompting Tabitha to say, "Never mind him, Phyl. His time is coming. He just doesn't know it yet."

Michael smiled to himself. Little did they know, he thought, and went to greet his first patient.

EVERY TIME MICHAEL DROVE to Tessie's home on Lake Minnetonka, he could feel a sense of calmness wash over him. There was something to be said about going home, especially when that home was located on one of the state's largest lakes in a sleepy little town nearly surrounded by water.

When Tessie and her husband had first built the house, it had been one of the many charming waterfront cottages dotting the shoreline. As the metropolitan area of Minneapolis and St. Paul had spread westward, the region had changed from a vacation resort to a residential community.

Now it was a playground for visitors, plus home to many who were fortunate enough to have one of the residences on the waterfront. Tessie was one of those residents living in a lake community yet having access to the city.

After knocking on her door and getting no answer, Michael reached into his pocket for his keys and let himself into the house.

"Tessie?" he called out, his voice resonating in the large, open hallway. He poked his head into the parlor, but she wasn't sitting in her favorite chair—a rocker he'd given her for her birthday a few years back. As he crossed the foyer, an Abyssinian cat slinked across the tiled floor, meowing as she rubbed up against his legs.

He bent to scratch her neck. "Hey, Cleo. How's life treating you?"

After a couple more meows, the cat slunk away. Michael guessed that Tessie was in the kitchen, for the aroma of pot roast tickled his nose. "Tessie?" he called out again, but still there was no answer.

He soon discovered she wasn't busy at work preparing dinner. Although wonderful aromas permeated the kitchen, and numerous pots sat on the stove, Tessie was nowhere in sight.

The back door, however, was open. He stepped outside and made a quick survey of the yard. He saw the patio, where wicker furniture sat empty. Geraniums hung from the eaves of the gazebo, but the chairs inside were vacant. The sandy beach was empty, the bench at the end of the dock held no one. Finally he looked toward the flower garden that stretched the entire length of the yard. There he caught a glimpse of a wide-brimmed sun hat, but it slipped around the corner of the house.

"Tessie?" he called out, and the hat came back into full view.

A smiling Tessie waved her gloved hand and smiled. "Oh, you're here already! I'll be right there," she called out to him, and disappeared momentarily before emerging with an armful of lilacs.

Watching her scoot across the yard caused a smile to appear on Michael's face. For a woman of eighty-one, she was extremely agile and full of energy. Although her hair was as white as snow, there was nothing else about Tessie McFerrin that identified her as an octogenarian. She had a zest for life few women half her age possessed.

When she reached the back stoop, she motioned for him to bend so she could give him a hug and a kiss. "Happy Birthday, Michael. I'm so glad you're spending it with me."

"Me, too," he told her, opening the back door for her. "Dinner smells wonderful."

"It's pot roast."

He smiled. "I thought so." She'd made it for him every year on his birthday ever since he could remember.

"It's a lot of food for just two people," she said as they stepped into the kitchen. "You should have brought a friend."

"You're the only one I want to be with on my birthday, Tessie. You know that."

She carried the lilacs over to the sink where a cut crystal vase sat on the counter. As she filled the vase with water, she said, "Has it been a nice birthday so far?"

"Yes, I've had a very nice day," he told her, which wasn't exactly the truth, but it wasn't a lie, either. Just because he didn't want to celebrate his birthday didn't mean he should tell her that. He couldn't tell her that, not after all the preparations she'd made. "They had a cake for me at the office."

"I knew they were going to. Tabitha called and said they were going to throw you a surprise party, but I told her that it wouldn't be a good idea."

"Thank you for saying that. You know I'm not fond of birthdays."

She set the flowers on the dining room table. "I know. That's why I didn't make a cake. I made pie. Lemon meringue."

Another of his favorites. "You shouldn't spoil me."

She smiled innocently as she walked past him.

"You're fun to spoil. I'm surprised some other woman hasn't discovered that by now."

He let the remark slip without commenting. In recent months she'd been mentioning his single status more often. Michael thought it was probably because the older she became, the more she worried about him not having someone to share his life with after she was gone.

As she tied an apron around her waist, he said, "Is there anything I can do to help?"

She gave him a gentle shove toward the dining room. "It's your birthday. You sit while I dish it up. It won't take me but a few minutes."

"But I want to help," he insisted.

"Then open the wine and pour us each a glass," she instructed. "There's a bottle of white zinfandel chilling in the dining room."

When he walked into the dining room, he saw the wine bucket with the bottle inside. He also noticed that there were not one but two pies cooling on the sideboard. When Tessie carried in a platter of pot roast with potatoes and vegetables, he asked, "Do we each get a pie for dessert?"

"As long as I was making one I thought I might as well make two. You never know when you'll get unexpected company," she answered innocently.

"You didn't *invite* anyone over tonight, did you?"

"Of course not," she answered quickly, then disappeared into the kitchen again.

When she returned, she carried the bun warmer and a large bowl of salad. "I think that's about it," she said, untying the apron from around her waist. "Shall we sit down?"

He held her chair for her, then after she was settled,

took his own spot to her right. Before eating, she reached for his hand and covered it with hers. "I feel very blessed, Michael, to be able to celebrate another birthday with you, although you should be celebrating with someone young and pretty."

"On this day, it wouldn't seem right to spend it anywhere but here with you." He lifted her hands to his lips and brushed a kiss across her knuckles. "I owe you so much."

"You don't owe me, Michael. When love is given, it should be given freely, not with expectations of getting something in return. You've brought me such great joy...." she paused, as emotion choked her throat. She pulled her hand out of his and reached for the handkerchief in her pocket. "This is a happy occasion, not a sad one," she said, dabbing at her eyes with the embroidered white linen cloth. "So no more of this schmaltz. Let's have a nice dinner together and you can tell me what your day was like at the clinic."

Michael did use his work as dinner conversation, knowing that Tessie loved animals as much as he did. If there was one person who understood his passion for his work, it was Tessie, and she'd always encouraged him to follow his dream of becoming a vet.

It was a nice way to spend one's birthday and the way he'd spent all of his—or at least the ones he could remember. He'd arrived at the McFerrin home when he was only four. Tessie and her husband had been taking in foster children most of their married life. Shortly before Michael had arrived, they'd decided to put their efforts into doing other types of volunteer work.

But then a friend of Tessie's had told her about Michael. Only four years old, he needed a place to stay while his mother waited for her trial to begin. As soon as Tessie had taken one look at him, she'd convinced Frank that they should take in one more foster child. When Michael's mother had been sentenced to a long prison term, Frank agreed with Tessie that they would provide a home for him as long as it was necessary.

Little did anyone know that Michael's birth mother would die of pneumonia while serving her sentence. When that happened, Tessie convinced Frank to adopt Michael, since there were no other living relatives. Michael had been a McFerrin for less than a year when Frank had a massive coronary and Tessie was left to raise him alone.

"I'd like to propose a toast," she said, raising her wineglass in the air. "To another year of good health and happiness in your work." She clinked her glass against his, then took a sip of the wine. "Now, when you've finished eating, I have a surprise for you."

"You weren't supposed to buy me a birthday present. I don't need anything but your love," he said, reaching across to squeeze her hand.

She smiled. "That's very sweet of you to say, but I happen to disagree."

He simply returned her smile and decided to graciously accept the shirt and tie she'd probably spent an afternoon finding for him. Only he soon discovered it wasn't a gift of clothing that she'd purchased for him. When they'd finished eating, she handed him an envelope.

"Go ahead. Open it. It won't bite," she teased as he hesitated.

She had such an expectant look of joy on her face, he knew he couldn't say another word but had to simply open the card and pretend to be thrilled. He guessed it contained a gift certificate to his favorite men's clothing store.

It didn't. Inside was an invitation to dinner. Michael glanced at Tessie, who was watching him for his reaction. "Dinner at eight on Saturday?"

She nodded excitedly.

"But with whom?"

"That's the surprise," Tessie told him with a gleeful glint in her eye.

"You've arranged for me to have dinner with someone," he repeated the obvious.

"Seven people, actually," she confessed.

Puzzled, he frowned, trying to figure out what she had planned. Then it hit him. It was probably dinner with seven of the Mums, the ladies his mother met with regularly on the pretext of discussing gardening, but he knew that they were more than a garden club. They were friends. Friends who wanted to help him celebrate his birthday.

A smile slowly spread across his face. "So you are giving me a party, after all," he said in a knowing tone.

"Oh, no. It's not a birthday party. It's a dinner," she corrected him.

"By any chance is it a dinner with some lovely ladies?" he asked with a sly smile.

"Yes, it is." She regarded him cautiously. "Did one of the girls let the secret out of the bag? Louella promised me she wouldn't say anything when she took Toby in for his shots."

"Louella didn't say anything," he reassured her.

"Then how did you know?" Now she was the one looking totally confused.

He reached across the table to pat her hand. "I didn't. I'm just a good guesser."

She looked a bit apologetic as she said, "It's not what you wanted, is it?"

"It's a lovely surprise."

"You think so?"

"Yes. I would be happy to have dinner with you and the Mums—provided you make sure they understand that it's not a birthday party."

Her brows drew close together. "The Mums?"

"Yes. You said seven ladies. They *are* the ones you've arranged for me to take to dinner, right?"

She gasped. "Oh, no. I wouldn't give you the Mums for your birthday." Then she began to laugh and, by the time her laughter was over, she had to remove her glasses and dab at her eyes with her handkerchief.

"What's so funny about the Mums wanting to have dinner with me?" he demanded.

"That's not what's so funny," she told him. As if it was too much for her, she reached for her water glass. "It's just that…well, they know about your birthday present and when they hear that you read the invitation and thought it was them…" Again she giggled.

"Just what *is* my birthday present?" he asked.

"Maybe you should finish reading your invitation." She reached over and tapped the embossed paper with her fingernail. "You didn't open it. You just read the front."

Michael picked it up and flipped it open. Inside was a note that read, "Happy Birthday, Michael. I hope you appreciate the gift your mother has given you and will join us for dinner at eight." It was signed by a woman named Claudia Dixon, Director.

Puzzled, he asked, "Director of what?"

"Dinner Date. She's a wonderful woman. So warm and sincere. Doing business with her was a real joy."

Uneasiness rumbled inside him. "Business? What kind of business?"

"Arranging dinners for people."

"Then this..." He glanced at the invitation again and saw the small logo at the bottom. "This Dinner Date is a service to arrange dinners?"

"Yes. Isn't it a lovely idea?"

"If you need help with that, then it's probably a valuable service." He reached over to take her hand in his. "But I wish you would have saved your money. You don't need to arrange a dinner party for me. Your dinners are special enough for me."

"But this isn't about having a dinner party, Michael. It's about meeting people."

Suspicion began to unfurl inside him. "Who will be at this dinner exactly? If you didn't invite the Mums, who *are* we going to be meeting?"

"Not *we,* Michael, *you.* You shouldn't be spending an evening with an old lady like me. You need to be with young people," she said with a twinkle in her eye.

He closed his eyes briefly. Oh no. She'd gone and done what she'd threatened to do for the past ten years. Set him up with the eligible women in town— or at least the ones she knew about. He knew Louella had a granddaughter who was single and so did Edith Larson. And then there was the woman who'd been giving her piano lessons.

He needed to get out of this dinner, but how could

he do it without hurting her feelings? "Mom, I'm going to feel a bit self-conscious if I'm the only man with seven women…" he began.

She chuckled. "Oh, you won't be the only man. There'll be four women and four men. Claudia knows her business."

"What men and what women?"

"Oh, I don't know that," she said cheerfully.

"Wait a minute." He straightened in his chair, uneasiness creeping along his nerves like a fog rolling in from the ocean. "How can you not know who you invited to dinner?"

"Because I didn't invite them. Claudia did. That's her job."

Michael picked up the dinner invitation and looked again at the logo. It said, "Dinner Date—bringing people together." Tessie had said there'd be four men and four women. This Claudia was bringing men and women together.

"Mother, please tell me this isn't a dating service," he said, a sick feeling in his stomach.

"It's not," she denied emphatically. "Dinner Date is an alternative to dating services. Instead of having to pay a lot of money, fill out all sorts of questionnaires, and then have someone 'choose' you as a prospective date, you simply go to dinner with a group of people who have similar interests as you. There's no matchmaking at all," she assured him quickly.

"Isn't the whole thing a matchmaking setup?"

"No, it isn't," she told him. "Claudia told me she started her business so that young professionals could enjoy an evening of dinner and good conversation without any of the pressures of dating. It's simply a way to meet other professionals your age."

"I have plenty of friends who make great dinner companions." It was true. He'd never lacked for female companionship. Tessie, however, didn't know that. Just because he never brought any of his lady friends to meet her, however, didn't mean they didn't exist.

"I'm sure you do." She patronized him by patting his hand. "I didn't purchase this opportunity for you because I thought you were short of friends. I just wanted to give you a chance to meet some nice young ladies...."

"I have women friends. I know it doesn't look like it, but I do date," he tried to convince her, but he could see by the lift of her eyebrows and the tilt of her chin that she didn't believe him.

"You haven't brought a single one here to meet me," she reminded him.

"If I bring one over does that mean you'll get a refund from this Claudia person?"

"That's not funny, Michael."

He hadn't meant it to be but didn't have the heart to tell her that. He struggled to find the right words. "I'm not much for dinners with strangers, Mom."

"It's simply an opportunity to meet people with similar interests as you."

"I don't think I'll meet them through some dating service."

"You don't know that, Michael. Louella says that her cousin Margaret's son Dennis—you know, the one who's the optometrist? Well, he was skeptical, just like you. But he went to Dinner Date and guess what?" She paused, waiting for him to ask what.

He didn't.

"He met a nice young accountant and they're planning to get married next year."

He could feel his collar tightening. "That's fine for Louella's cousin's whatever..." He trailed off impatiently. "But I like to choose my own dates."

"This isn't a date," she corrected him. "It's simply an opportunity to have dinner and meet new people." She got to her feet to go over to the bureau. She pulled a pamphlet from the drawer and gave it to him. "Here. You can read about it for yourself."

Michael took one look at the Dinner Date brochure and set it aside with a grimace. "I really don't want to read about it."

"You don't want my gift to you?" From the look of horror on her face, Michael would have thought he'd asked her to put dear old Cleo to sleep.

He wanted to say no, that he wasn't going to go to any arranged dinner of single people, but there was something about the look in her eyes that stopped him. He raked a hand across the back of his neck. "I hate the thought of you spending money on something like this."

"But this is the way I *want* to spend my money," she assured him. "You work far too many nights and weekends, helping this one or helping that one," she said with a flourish of her hand in midair. "Please let me give you a nice evening out with young people your own age. Just one dinner where you can talk to others who share your interests."

He wanted to refuse. Going to dinner with seven strangers who were looking for love through a dating service was not how he wanted to spend a Saturday evening. Yet Tessie never asked for much. She'd raised him ever since he was a small boy, giving him the love and care his own mother hadn't been able to give to him. How could he say no?

"I really wish you hadn't spent your money on this," he said, tapping the side of the invitation against the table.

"It's worth it if it makes you happy," she said, coming over to give him a kiss on the cheek.

Only it didn't make him happy, yet he couldn't tell her that. She'd been so excited to give him the gift. She had no idea how much he disliked the idea.

"You *are* going to go to the dinner, aren't you?"

Every instinct inside him wanted him to say no, but before he could say another word, there was a knock at the door.

"I wonder who that could be?" Tessie said aloud, looking as if she knew exactly who was at the door.

Michael's glance flew to the sideboard. "Probably someone who heard you'd baked two pies."

She flitted out of the room. When she returned she was accompanied by half a dozen gray-haired women. The Mums had arrived.

To Michael's dismay, they came with a gift. After greeting each of them and receiving more birthday hugs, he opened the package. Inside was a shirt and tie.

"For your dinner on Saturday," Louella told him with a twinkle in her eye.

Michael almost said, "I'm not going to dinner on Saturday," but the group of women gathered around him were the dearest ladies he knew. They'd been mothering him almost as long as Tessie had been.

So instead of telling them he could get a date without their help, he simply said, "Thank you. This will make me look like a man about town."

They all smiled and ate their lemon meringue pie. Michael knew his chances of getting out of the dinner were between slim and next to none. But Lynn was going on vacation, which meant he'd be the vet on call next weekend.

Maybe there was hope.

Chapter Two

Normally the clinic was open until three on Saturdays. Oftentimes that wasn't near long enough. Pets—like humans—frequently needed treatment on weekends after the office was closed and Michael did his best to accommodate them.

Only on this particular Saturday, business was very slow. As the hands on the clock moved toward closing time, he knew that unless an emergency arose, he wasn't going to be able to use work as an excuse for not going to the dinner Tessie had arranged. Nor could he say he lost track of time and forgot. His mother called him at least four times to remind him of her birthday gift.

"It's certainly been a quiet Saturday, hasn't it?" Tabitha commented as she sprayed disinfectant over the surgical table. "Hope that doesn't mean you're going to have a crazy night. You are on call, right?"

Michael nodded. "Lynn's out of town for the weekend."

"Well, let's hope you're lucky and you can enjoy what's left of yours without any interruptions."

Little did she know that an interruption was exactly what he needed. Unsure of how to approach the subject, he said, "I was wondering if you could do me a favor this evening?"

"What kind of favor?"

"Could you page me at eight o'clock?"

"I guess, but why?" She fixed him with a perplexed stare.

"Let's just say I'm in a bit of a predicament that I need to get out of without hurting anybody's feelings."

"Oh, I get it. I'll page you and you'll go to a phone, pretend to call and then announce to whoever it is you're with that you have to leave. Is that it?" A sly twinkle danced in her eye.

He felt like a fool for having to ask, especially because he could see by the look on her face that she thought he'd gotten himself involved with a woman and didn't know how to extricate himself.

He debated as to whether or not he should tell her the truth. Tabitha had been a loyal employee for six years, yet he was not naive enough to believe she didn't talk with the other women in the office.

"That's it. And it's not what you're thinking."

"It isn't?"

"No. It's..." He paused, then finally decided to take the risk, and said, "The only reason I'm asking you to do this is because of Tessie." He went on to explain her birthday gift to him, expecting her to find it amusing.

"What a sweet thing to do. I hear dating services are very popular and a great way to meet people."

"Then you don't see anything wrong with using one?"

"No, not at all." She smiled. "Although I have to admit in your case it is kind of funny that Tessie thinks you need help getting a date. Obviously she doesn't know about…''

''No, she doesn't. So you can see why I need you to page me at eight. I really don't want to go to anything connected with a dating service.''

''But you can't hurt her feelings.''

''Exactly.''

''Very well, boss. At eight o'clock I'll ring your pager. Anything else you want before I leave?''

''I would appreciate you not mentioning this to anyone else…for Tessie's sake, of course.''

''Of course. It's our secret.'' She made a gesture as if she had an imaginary key locking her lips.

Michael didn't like secrets. They had a way of slipping out when one least expected it, but he was relieved he'd talked to Tabitha. Now he could put in an appearance at the dinner and make Tessie happy. He smiled to himself and patted the pager he had clipped to his belt.

Later that evening as he parked his Ford Explorer outside the popular five-star restaurant, it suddenly occurred to him that he was going to be in a very public place and might be recognized. He groaned silently. What he didn't need was for his friends to learn that he'd gone to a dating service dinner.

He decided to stay in the car for as long as he could to avoid that possibility. He sat listening to the radio, watching other patrons go inside. Every time he saw a single man or woman, he wondered if they were one of the hopeless. For that's how he viewed his dinner companions. Despite Tabitha's assurances that dating services had changed and were now an acceptable option as a meeting place for singles, he couldn't help but regard them as playgrounds of the hopeless.

He watched as the numbers on the digital clock continued to change with each passing minute until he knew he could put off the inevitable no longer. Reluctantly he climbed out of the car and went inside.

At the hostess stand, an attractive blonde wearing a very short skirt and a glittery tight top eyed him with obvious interest as he approached. "One for dinner?"

"Actually I'm meeting some people. I believe the reservation is under Claudia Dixon," he answered, wishing he could say he was alone. Even eating alone in a fancy restaurant on a Saturday night was preferable to the ordeal he was about to endure.

"You're with Dinner Date?" The blonde lifted one eyebrow with definite interest and her smile became even friendlier. "Claudia said she had a unique group coming in tonight, but she didn't tell me it would have so many attractive men in it."

"You want to join us for dinner?" Michael asked, not one to pass up an opportunity to flirt.

She gave him an equally flirtatious grin as she said, "Wish I could, but duty calls. However, maybe if you're still here when I get off…" She let the sentence dangle.

"Maybe." He gave her a promising smile, knowing perfectly well that he would be gone before she had time to rest her pretty little feet.

She looked down at the book in front of her. "You must be Michael." She scribbled over his name with a pen, then looked up and gave him another smile. "Follow me and I'll show you where everybody is."

As he followed her swaying hips, he wished that

she was going to be included in the dinner party, but then he realized that the hostess was not the kind of woman that needed anyone to find her an escort. Which only made him wonder again about the men and women who would be at this dinner.

Unsuitable was the first word that came to mind. Normally he didn't prejudge people, but in this case, he honestly didn't see what he would have in common with anyone who thought a dating service was necessary to find a date.

Tessie had said the men and women who used Dinner Date were professionals. Professional duds was probably a better description, he thought as each step took him closer to his destination.

"You have a very nice table in the back, very private," the blonde told him as she escorted him through the dining area.

Michael didn't comment, but continued to follow her until he caught a glimpse of his dinner companions. They were seated at a round table. He stopped when he saw that all of the chairs had occupants.

The hostess, however, continued toward the table, bending to say something to a woman with red hair, who immediately jumped up when she saw him.

With hand outstretched, she came toward him. "Hi. I'm Claudia Dixon. You must be Michael."

He shook her outstretched hand, wishing he had never accepted Tessie's gift. He should have simply told his mother that as much as he loved her, he didn't want to have dinner with a bunch of strangers.

"Come. I'll introduce you to the others," Claudia said, pulling him by the arm over to the table.

The others were all thirty-something professionals who readily shook his hand and smiled warmly as he was introduced to each of them individually. Everyone was identified by first name and occupation. Michael heaved a sigh of relief when he didn't recognize a single face.

Although all four of the women were attractive, Michael didn't expect that he'd be asking for any phone numbers at the end of the evening. Not that he could have. As Claudia explained, if anyone wanted to pursue a friendship with any of the participants, protocol required that it be done through Dinner Date. Phone numbers would only be given out through the service and that would only happen if the other person agreed to another meeting.

Michael took his seat between two women and listened as Claudia explained that twice during the meal—after the appetizers had been served and just before dessert—the women would move over one chair in order that everyone had an opportunity to visit with everybody at the dinner. She encouraged them to get to know one another and have a pleasant evening.

"Since my work is done, I'll leave you to get acquainted. I know you're going to enjoy this evening and hope that you'll recommend Dinner Date to other singles."

Not likely, Michael thought, tempted to loosen the tie that felt as if it were choking him. He still couldn't believe that he was here and, for the umpteenth time, wished that he hadn't accepted Tessie's gift. As he glanced around the table he expected that the others would look as uncomfortable as he felt.

To his surprise, however, very few looked uneasy. He wondered if it was because everyone in this room had done this type of thing before. Maybe they were used to being in a small group and having to break the ice. Or maybe they were extroverts. Or maybe they were all just really lonely and welcomed the opportunity to talk to strangers.

"Is this your first time?" Sharon, the nurse on his right, asked him.

"As a matter of fact it is," he replied. He wanted to tell her—and the entire group—just why he was sitting at the dinner table with them. He mentally debated whether he should make an announcement, let them know his motives were not the same as theirs. What he didn't need was for any of the women to think he was seriously looking for a mate.

Because he wasn't.

Sharon, however, obviously was, judging by the way she was looking at him. "So you're an animal doctor," she said, studying him intently.

"Yes."

"That's probably why Claudia put us next to each other. We're both in health care," she said with a smile that implied they shared a secret. "What do you like to do in your free time?"

"I have very little free time," he answered.

"Which is why it's so hard to meet people." She drew her own conclusion as to why he was there. "I know that feeling."

To his relief, the appearance of a waitress preempted any further conversation. As she passed out menus and took beverage orders, Michael asked for a Scotch on the rocks.

Although the waitress didn't bat an eyelash upon hearing his request, he could see that the others weren't expecting him to order an alcoholic beverage. After hearing everyone else at the table order coffee, tea or a soft drink, he turned to Sharon and asked, "Are we not supposed to drink at these things?"

"Claudia puts nondrinkers together," she answered. "Did you check the wrong box on the application form?"

He hadn't checked any box. That was the problem. Here he was at a dinner with people who supposedly had similar interests as he did—or in this case, as Tessie thought he had. He sighed. What had she gotten him into?

Again the urge to announce to the table exactly why he was having dinner with them was great. Except what would he say? That he was only here because his mother made him come? Good grief. He was thirty-five, not thirteen. No, these people wouldn't understand why he'd attend a dinner simply to please his mother. It was better to say nothing and stick it out until Tabitha called. Then he could beat feet out of the restaurant and never return.

If there was one thing the Scotch on the rocks had done it was to get Sharon the nurse to turn her attention to the man on her right. Michael took a sip of the amber liquid, needing the hot, burning sensation it created as he swallowed it. As he set his glass down, he noticed a pair of eyes on him.

They belonged to a woman Claudia had introduced as Cassie and held a sparkle of amusement in them. She smiled at him and said, "So tell me, what's it like being an animal doctor, Dr. Michael?"

He liked the sound of her voice. It was low and sultry—more like something he'd find in a lounge singer. A direct contrast to the fair skin and mischievous sparkle in her blue eyes.

"Probably quite different from an artist's life," he

answered. Before he could say another word, the man to her right interrupted, changing the subject and capturing the artist's attention.

Michael continued to watch her, surprised by the ease with which she managed to converse with a table of strangers. His initial impression that she was rather shy had obviously been wrong. Of all the guests at the dinner, she looked as if talking with strangers was a joy, not an anxiety.

Although the man to her right tried to monopolize her attention, she managed to include several of the guests in their conversation. Michael thought both men on either side of her appeared to be a bit smitten. Not that Michael blamed them. She was like a painting. The first time you looked at her you saw a pleasant scene, but the longer you stared, the more beautiful she became.

She had a rather free-spirited look to her, with her long, straight blond hair and pale skin. Her eyes weren't warm, yet there was something about them that begged for you to try to understand the woman behind them. She wore very little makeup compared to the woman he usually dated, but then she didn't need any. Her skin was as smooth as the petals found on the flowers in Tessie's garden.

Michael found himself staring at her and becoming more intrigued with each passing moment. Although there was steady conversation on his side of the table, he repeatedly found himself glancing across the table and meeting the blue eyes of Cassie, the artist. And every time he did, those eyes would regard him with a glint of amusement that made him think she knew exactly how uncomfortable he was sitting there.

Although there were moments when the conversation included all eight guests at the table, most of the talk was between people sitting next to each other. That, however, didn't keep Michael from listening to what others said. He tuned in specifically to what Cassie was saying. She was a skillful conversationalist, saying very little about herself yet gleaning information from others. It only made him more curious about her.

Everything about her was graceful. From the way her head tilted ever so slightly on her beautiful, swan-like neck, to the manner with which she ate her escargots. He found himself wondering just what kind of art she did with those long, slender fingers. But more than that, he wondered why she was looking for love through a dating service.

As the appetizer plates were cleared away, he found himself wishing that it had been the main course they'd just finished, because the women would once more move over a chair and Cassie would be next to him. But during the main course, his pager buzzed. He realized it was eight o'clock. Tabitha was right on schedule.

Intrigued by the artist and wanting the opportunity to talk to her when she moved next to him, he didn't call his assistant. When the last of the dinner plates had been taken away, Cassie announced that it was once again time to change places.

She took the chair next to Michael's right and gave him the same furtive smile she'd cast his way when he'd ordered the Scotch. "So, Dr. Michael. You never did answer my question. What's it like being an animal doctor?"

"It's a challenge," he answered honestly, noticing that she had a tiny dimple in one cheek that wasn't noticeable until you were close to her. "And please, call me Mac."

"And do you like challenges, Dr. Mac?" she asked provocatively.

"Yes. Aren't they the spice of life?"

"No, that's variety."

"I like that, too," he answered with an equally flirtatious grin. "And what about you? What's it like being an artist?"

"It's incredibly frustrating."

"Really?"

She nodded. "Mmm-hmm. Perfection is never easy to achieve."

"And you strive for perfection when you paint?"

"Oh, it's not my work that is perfect. It's my subjects. Trying to reproduce beauty is in many ways a challenge, too."

"Then we have something in common, don't we?"

"Professionally, anyway."

"What about the personal Cassie? What does she like to do when she's not meeting the frustrating challenges of capturing beauty?"

"My art is my life," she answered with a candor that surprised him. He expected some flirtatious banter, but instead she was sincere. "That doesn't mean I work twenty-four hours a day," she was quick to add. "But I do tend to get so involved with a project that I lose track of time."

"That sounds like a warning."

She smiled, another furtive grin. "Now why would I need to warn you, Dr. Mac?"

"Maybe because you know that all evening I've been sitting here waiting for you to finally come sit in that chair."

She lifted both brows in a provocative invitation. "I'm here."

"Yes, and I'm glad." He leaned closer to her so that only she would hear his next words. "I've always thought dessert was the best part of a meal." She laughed, a wonderful, throaty sound that did funny things to Michael's insides.

"Then we have something else in common, don't we?" she said, and picked up her fork and cut into the slice of cheesecake.

"Oh, I think we might have a quite a few things in common," he said.

"Such as?"

"A mutual love of nature."

"And how do you know I love nature?"

"You do, don't you?"

She smiled. "Yes, but doesn't everyone?"

"Not the way you and I do. Others see rain and think it's a nuisance. You and I don't see rain. We smell it. We taste it. We hear it. We feel it."

"Are you sure you're a doctor and not a poet?" She reached for her water glass. Before she could raise it to her lips, he tapped it with his. "To challenge."

She clinked her glass against his and smiled that provocative grin of hers. "To challenge."

He couldn't believe how well things were going. She again asked him about his work and he entertained her with anecdotes from the clinic. It was as if the other six people ceased to exist. All he wanted was to hear that luscious, sultry voice of hers and see that sly, flirtatious smile.

Then his pager buzzed again.

"Oh-oh. Looks like Dr. Mac in on call," she remarked.

He pushed his sport coat aside and reached for the electronic device. It was his escape route. Only now he didn't need or want a way out of the dinner.

"I think this thing is malfunctioning," he told her, clicking the button that revealed Tabitha's number. "I'm getting a scrambled message."

"Do you need to check with your service?"

"No, it's all right. I'm sure it was nothing." But only a few minutes later the pager buzzed again. As he read Tabitha's number, he wondered why she hadn't given up? Surely she could figure out that if he hadn't answered the pager, it meant he was having a good time and didn't need to make his escape?

"You have to go, don't you?" Cassie said, the disappointment in her voice making it all the more difficult to leave.

He wanted to ignore the page, but he also knew that it could very well be an emergency. In all good conscience, he couldn't disregard any attempt that might be a call for help. Reluctantly he folded his napkin and laid it on the table.

"I'd better go check and make sure this isn't something important. Don't go away. I'll be right back."

Instead of going out to the car to use his cell phone, he used the pay phone in the lobby. He punched in the seven digits of Tabitha's home phone number.

He knew she had caller ID when she said, "How come you're calling from a pay phone?"

"Because I didn't want to bring the cell phone into the restaurant."

"Well, for someone who was itching to get out of

dinner, it sure took you a long time to answer your page.''

He didn't want to tell her that he'd met Cassie and was no longer in a hurry to make a hasty departure from the dinner.

''Mookie's in labor and it doesn't look good. I think she needs a cesarean.''

Mookie was Tabitha's mother's schnauzer. ''You've seen her?''

''Mom brought her over here because she was acting strange. I put her in the basement and left her alone, but it's obvious she's having big troubles, Mac. You'd better hurry.''

''I'm on my way,'' he told her, then hung up the phone. He hurried back to the private dining room and bent so that he could speak to Cassie.

''I have to go. It's an emergency.''

''Another challenge?''

''Yes, but I'd much prefer the one right here,'' he said softly. ''I'd like to get to know Cassie the artist. Maybe we could do that when there weren't so many people around?'' He could see the curious glance of Sharon the nurse and didn't doubt for a moment that she was straining to hear every word of their private conversation.

Coyly, Cassie answered, ''You know the rules, Dr. Mac.''

''Call Claudia at Dinner Date,'' he stated in understanding. ''You can be sure I will.'' Then he made a formal apology to the group and left.

As he drove the distance to Tabitha's home, his thoughts were of Cassie the artist. First thing Monday morning he was going to call Dinner Date. He definitely wanted to get to know her better. And judging by the way she had smiled, she wanted the same thing. Oh, Tessie was going to be happy.

"CASSIE, IT'S CLAUDIA. If you're there, pick up."

Normally Cassandra Carrigan didn't answer her phone when she was in her studio, but she'd been having difficulty concentrating on her work all morning and the call was a distraction she welcomed. She set her paintbrush aside and reached for the telephone.

"I'm here. What's up?" she asked, dispensing with the routine hello. She and Claudia had been friends far too long to worry about greetings.

"You have to quit flirting. You're way too good at your job. I still have men calling from dinners you worked months ago."

"I don't flirt," she said, smiling to herself. "I'm friendly."

Claudia made a sound of disbelief. "You flirt and the guys love it. That's why I'm always delighted when you say you'll work a dinner. Tell me about Saturday night."

"It was an interesting group," she answered, even though her thoughts for the past two days had focused on only one interesting man in that group. Dr. Mac, the veterinarian.

He didn't look like a vet. More like a stockbroker. Clean-cut. Intelligent brow, strong, determined nose that looked as if it may have once been broken. Wonderful smile with straight, even teeth. But it was his eyes that had caught Cassie's attention. They were round with just a fraction of white visible below the dark iris, which showed he possessed great sensitivity.

Which she was certain he used to his advantage. He had used his charm on her and even she, with all her practice, had nearly fallen for it. She had a feeling, however, that he was just another good-looking guy looking for an ornament to dangle from his arm. She'd met quite a few of them through the dating service.

"Sounds as if everyone had a good time," Claudia remarked.

"So you should be happy I did my job well," she pointed out. "It's what you want me to do, isn't it? Keep the conversation going?"

"Yes, it is, and I know you can't help but be your usual charming self, but this time three of the four men from Saturday night requested another meeting with you."

"Three?" That was unusual. Maybe one or, sometimes on the rare occasion, two would request another date with her, but three? "You did tell them I don't share their interest, right?"

"Of course I did and two of them understood, but there was one who refused to take no for an answer. He says you told him you wanted to see him again."

"Now *that* I know I didn't do," she answered honestly. "And you know I didn't, either. The only reason I attend the dinners is because I enjoy dining out and being with people who are interesting."

Claudia sighed. "I don't know how you do it, Cassie."

"Do what?"

"Meet so many good-looking men and not get the least bit interested in any of them."

"It's just a job, Claudia."

"But aren't you even the least bit curious to hear who it is that wants to get to know you better?"

She was. The memory of Dr. Mac, the veterinarian,

smiling into her face and telling her he liked a challenge popped into her head. Part of her wanted it to be him, the other part didn't.

"I'm not interested in dating anyone. You know that."

"I do, but I keep thinking that one of these times you'll forget that you're doing a job and simply enjoy yourself."

"I do enjoy myself," she insisted.

"So do you want to know which client won't stop asking about you?"

Cassie groaned. "All right. Tell me."

"It's Michael the veterinarian."

At the mention of his name, she felt a tiny shiver travel up and down her spine. "Oh, it *was* Dr. Mac," she said more to herself than to her friend.

"You don't sound surprised."

"Maybe I did go a bit overboard with the flirting, but not once did I say I wanted to see him again. I told him what I tell all the men I meet—that if he's interested he should contact you."

"He took that as a yes."

Her heart fluttered at the thought. "Then you're going to have to convince him that it's a no."

"I tried to, but I didn't have much luck. What did you do to the guy?"

"Do? I didn't do anything," she answered. It would have been more accurate to say that he had done something to her. Ever since Saturday night he'd been occupying her thoughts far too much of the time, which was one of the reasons for her lack of concentration this morning. In the two years she'd worked for the dating service she hadn't met anyone who'd had that effect on her.

"What part of no doesn't he understand?" she asked a bit impatiently.

"It's nothing to get upset about," Claudia said in a soothing tone. "I said he was persistent, not obsessive."

She relaxed a bit. "You're right. We only used our first names so it's not like he can track me down, is it? And you've done background checks on all your clients."

"That's right. I just wanted to check with you before I throw a bucket of water on his ardor. He was rather cute, wasn't he?"

"I'm not sure 'cute' is the right word," she said evasively. "'Charming' would have been a better adjective. He's a player."

"You think so?"

"Yes. I wonder why he was at the dinner. Players usually don't need to use a dating service to find a companion."

Claudia didn't comment but asked, "Are you available for next Saturday?"

"Did he ask to attend another dinner with me?"

"Of course he asked, but you know I'd never do that. I wouldn't do it to a client and I certainly wouldn't do it to a friend." There was indignation in her friend's voice.

"I'm sorry, Claudia. I know you wouldn't. Sure, I'm available next Saturday."

They talked for another few minutes about matters totally unrelated to Dinner Date. By the time Cassie hung up the phone, she'd forgotten all about Dr. Mac.

Which was a good thing. The only reason she'd been able to accept the job with the dating service was because she truly could attend the dinners with a sense of detachment. She had no interest in meeting a suitable companion. No interest in dating. No interest in men.

A man like Dr. Mac had the potential of being able to change all of that. As she returned to her painting she was grateful that she'd never see him again.

"MOM! WHAT ARE YOU DOING HERE?" Michael asked when he stepped into examining room number four and saw Tessie sitting there.

"Cleo's not well," she answered, nodding toward the Abyssinian that sat curled up on her lap.

"She looks okay," he observed, lifting the purring cat from her lap.

"Oh, but she's not. She wouldn't eat this morning," she answered.

"Maybe she wasn't hungry," he said, placing Cleo on the examining table. "We all like to skip a meal now and then."

"Speaking of meals…" Tessie took her place next to him and watched as he did a routine exam. "You didn't call and let me know how the dinner went on Saturday."

So that was the true reason for the visit to the clinic. "It was fine. Just as Cleo is fine now."

"You're sure?"

"About the dinner or Cleo?" he quipped.

She clicked her tongue. "I know you're a good vet. If you say Cleo is fine, she's fine. Did you enjoy yourself at the dinner?"

"As a matter of fact I did," he answered, reaching for a cat treat.

He watched his mother's eyes light up at the

thought. She smiled smugly and said, "I knew you would."

"They served the most wonderful coq au vin. You would have loved it. The mushroom sauce was exquisite, prepared just the way you like it. And they had those little baby carrots in a wine sauce and escargots...you know how much I like escargots."

She fluttered her fingers nervously in midair. "I don't care about the food. Tell me about the people. Did you meet anyone interesting?"

"There was a very nice engineer who'd worked on that new overpass on the interstate right outside of downtown, you know, the one that opened in April. He had some very interesting observations."

Again her fingers flailed about in midair. "I don't care about the men at the dinner, Michael. Tell me about the women."

He shrugged. "There's not much to tell. They were nice."

She frowned. "Is that all you can find to say about them? They were nice?"

"Actually, there was one who was very nice." His mouth automatically split into a grin at the memory of Cassie the artist.

"Nice enough that you might have dinner with her again?"

He'd been debating whether or not he should tell her about Cassie the artist. Now that the opportunity had arrived, he decided the less said the better. "No. It was a very nice evening and I thank you."

"But what about the four women? They didn't share your interests?"

Again he thought of Cassie. "Not exactly," he

hedged. "Did you ever think that maybe none of them were attracted to me?"

Tessie gasped. "That's impossible! Look at you. You're the complete package."

He couldn't help but smile again, this time at her maternal defense of him. "Not everyone sees me through your eyes, Mom."

"I'm not just saying that because I'm your mother. Ask any of the Mums, they'll say the same thing." She shook her head in bemusement. "What is wrong with the youth of today? When a handsome young man like you has trouble getting a date…"

"I can find a date," he assured her.

She dismissed his comment with a flap of her hand. "You don't need to pretend with me. I know that you spend a lot of your free time alone."

Guilt washed over him. He hadn't been completely honest with Tessie over the years. He wasn't often without female companionship, yet Tessie was unaware of his love life. He'd deliberately kept it that way, because he hadn't wanted her getting attached to any of the women in his life, because he knew none of them would last.

"Mom, there are other places to meet women than through a dating service," he said gently.

"I know that, dear, but I had hoped that my gift would be a lasting one," she said on a sigh. "You're thirty-five, Michael, and I'm eighty-one. Time is running out."

He pulled her into his arms and gave her a hug. "Now you stop your worrying. We have plenty of time—both of us. Your birthday gift was unique and I haven't given up on finding a special lady."

She pushed him away. "You haven't?"

"No. If there's someone out there for me, I'll find her. You know that."

"You always have loved a challenge, haven't you?" she said with a knowing grin.

Yes, he did, and he didn't consider this one to be over yet.

Chapter Three

"We'll discuss old business first," Louella Gibbons addressed the Mums gathered around Betty Jean's dining room table. "We'll start with Dr. Mac, since Tessie has to leave early for a dentist appointment."

"Thank you, Lou." Tessie rose to her feet, clearing her throat. "By now you all know we didn't get the desired results we hoped for with Dinner Date."

The chorus of groans indicated that everyone was as disappointed as Tessie.

"Maybe we should try another one?" Edith suggested.

Tessie shook her head. "It's not cost-effective. We need another plan."

"I agree," Mildred spoke up. "*We* are better matchmakers than those dating services. I say we make up our own list of eligible young ladies and do our own matchmaking."

Several comments supporting Mildred's suggestion came at once.

Louella clapped her gavel. "One at a time, ladies, please."

"I think Mildred's right," Agnes said. "That's

what we did for Francine's granddaughter and look at those results.''

''She's happily married and expecting a baby and all because we sent her on a blind date with Betty Jean's cousin's grandson,'' Louella stated.

''But Michael refuses to go on a blind date,'' Tessie pointed out.

''Then we'll just have to get to know this girl ourselves and invite her to a Mum gathering that Michael plans to attend,'' Edith stated simply, as if it would be the easiest thing in the world to orchestrate.

''Do we have a young lady in mind?'' Louella asked.

''I do,'' Dorothy Sandberg said with a furtive twinkle in her eye. ''Her name is…''

''IT IS AN HONOR to have such a beautiful display of art in our center.''

Cassie accepted the compliment graciously, smiling at the gray-haired gentleman. ''I am the one who is honored, Emmet. I can't think of a better place to exhibit my work.''

''But you could have gone to any of the galleries in town and had your opening. For you to allow us to show these beautiful portraits here…well, it is very good for the center.''

''And you have been good to me,'' she acknowledged, appreciating the assistance the director of the senior citizen center had given her. From helping her find models to sit for her portraits to making the arrangements so that she could exhibit her work at the center, Emmet Sandberg had done everything he could to help her turn her dream into a reality.

''I've been looking at these pictures all morning

and I still haven't gotten tired of looking at them,'' he told her, his eyes making another survey of the room.

The pictures he referred to were portraits sketched by Cassie. Eighteen pastels of married couples. Two sketches—one as newlyweds, the other as they currently were in the golden years of their marriages. She'd titled the exhibit "Everlasting Love.''

"Thank you. That's one of the nicest compliments I could receive," she said sincerely.

"Did you know that when you add up the total number of years all of these people have been married, it comes to exactly one thousand?'' He didn't wait for her to answer, but said, "Dorothy figured it out.''

Dorothy was the woman in portrait number four, Emmet's wife of fifty-one years. At first she had been a bit reticent about posing for Cassie, but after sitting down to coffee and doughnuts and discovering that Cassie's grandmother had belonged to the same Sons of Norway lodge as Emmet and Dorothy, she'd become one of her staunchest supporters.

"You could have called this 'A Millennium of Love,''' Emmet continued. "Wouldn't that have been a great title?''

"It certainly would be accurate, wouldn't it?'' she answered. She didn't tell him that Dorothy had suggested the very same thing and on more than one occasion. With all the hype that had preceded the turn of the century, Cassie hadn't wanted to use the word *millennium* in connection with her work.

"These portraits aren't just about numbers,'' she told Emmet. "They're about people who have worked hard to keep marriages intact through loss and suffering. The faces in these pictures have had great joy, but they've also lived through wars and economic hardship. And despite all the social and political turmoil of the past century, their love has lasted.''

''Ah, that is so true,'' he said, a gnarly finger propped against his chin as he studied the portrait of a couple who'd been married seventy-two years. ''With those colored chalks of yours, you tell so much. The love, the joy, the wisdom…it's all there.'' He took several steps to his left until he stood in front of his own portrait. ''I mean, look at my Dorothy. When I look at the picture it's almost as if I can hear her saying 'Everything's going to be all right, Emmet.' You have a gift, Cassandra. You show the best of people.''

''I only draw what I see,'' Cassie told him. ''The emotions expressed here are not mine. I'm just the instrument for showing who these people really are, and each one is someone very special.''

''And I thank you for showing that to the world. Not many people would devote an entire exhibit of art to old people.''

''Well, I did, and I'm very glad that I took the time to get to know these wonderful married couples.'' She spread her arms in an encompassing gesture. ''They are my tribute to aging and to love that endures the test of time.''

She again surveyed the room, appreciating the lighting and the spacing of her portraits. Even though the center wasn't an art gallery, the staff had constructed a very elegant and artistic display of her work. It reinforced her decision to have the opening at the center rather than in an art gallery.

"You did a wonderful job arranging the portraits, Emmet," she complimented the older man.

He smiled. "I had help. My sister used to work at the Walker. Of course, she's retired now, but she has a good eye, don't you think?"

"Yes, I do. I'd like to meet her. Will she be here tonight?"

"As a matter of fact, she will. And so will lots of other people. It's going to be a wonderful opening."

"I'm sure it will be." Cassie had a rush of nervous excitement at the thought of a project so dear to her heart finally being ready for public display. "What time would you like me to be here?"

"Maybe an hour before opening…would that work for you? We've invited all of the married couples in the pictures to come early so they can see the exhibit before it's open to the public."

"Good. I'm looking forward to seeing them again."

"And they will be delighted to see you. Will you be bringing a guest?"

"Yes, I will. A friend of mine."

"Might I ask this friend's name…for a name tag, of course," he asked with a twinkle in his eyes.

"Her name is Claudia," Cassie answered, knowing perfectly well that Emmet was curious to know if she had a special man in her life. Every time she had sat down to begin another portrait, it never failed. She was asked the same question, "Are you married?"

And when she'd say that she wasn't, she'd get a similar response, something like, "I can't believe a beautiful girl like you is still single."

Then she'd mention that she was a widow and the bemusement would turn to sympathy, producing comments such as, "Oh, you poor girl...to have loved and to have lost...he wouldn't want you to be alone the rest of your life."

Emmet and Dorothy had been no different from the other seniors and she suspected that Emmet's curiosity about her guest this evening was spurred by his wife's interest. Something that was confirmed by his next statement.

"You're bringing a girlfriend." He sighed. "Dorothy will be disappointed. She'd hoped that by the time all of the portraits were finished you'd have a young man and your next exhibit might be newlywed love."

"No, I'm afraid I have no such plans," she said with an apologetic smile.

He reached for her hand. "Not to worry. You're young. You have plenty of time to make plans," he said consolingly.

Cassie didn't need to be consoled. She wasn't pining after her dead husband, nor was she longing for a second chance at love. She was comfortable with her single status, which was probably why she found the "Everlasting Love" project so fascinating. In an era when so many marriages failed, it was refreshing to work with those that had remained solidly intact for more than fifty years.

"I'd like to say maybe you'll meet some nice young man here tonight at the opening, but our guests this evening will probably all be senior citizens," Emmet told her with a look of regret.

"I can't think of a nicer group of people to share my work with on opening night," she remarked. She was grateful when he was paged by the office to take a phone call and the subject of her personal life could be set aside. Cassie gave him another smile, assured him she'd be on time this evening and waved goodbye.

While he was gone, she went over to the portrait with the number one beside it. It was of her own grandparents, William and Mary Carrigan. Little had she known at the time she had drawn them that it would be the inspiration for an entire project.

She looked at the happy faces smiling at her and felt all warm inside. They were such dear people and, like the others, happily married for over half a century.

"Sharing. That's the key to staying married," her grandfather had told her on more than one occasion. "Never keep anything from each other. You must be best friends and share everything."

Cassie sighed. She'd followed that advice during her short marriage to Darryl. Unfortunately, he hadn't. A tiny stinging sensation erupted in her chest and she determinedly pushed such thoughts aside.

No point in thinking about the past. It was gone. So was Darryl. She was happy. She had a life—not the life that these senior citizens in her portraits had, but a good, fulfilling life.

As she gave one last glance to the exhibit, she told herself that everlasting love was wonderful—for some people. But not everyone.

Not her. She sighed, then went home to shower and put on her opening night dress.

"DR. MAC, I HAVE that information you wanted." Tabitha handed him a small stack of papers. "Here's a listing of the art galleries in Minneapolis and St. Paul and their current exhibits by local artists."

"I didn't realize there'd be so many," he said, leafing through the stack. "Thank you. I'm sure this will be very helpful. I only hope it didn't take up too much of your time."

"Actually, it did, but if you clue me in on why you need this information, I'll forgive you," she said with an impish grin.

Michael debated just how much he should tell his assistant. "I'm looking for a particular artist, that's all."

"Would this be a female artist by chance?"

He grinned. "As a matter of fact, it is. Satisfied?"

"So you want to go see her work, is that it?"

"I am curious to see it, yes," he admitted.

"If you had given me her name, I could have eliminated all the paperwork," she said, nodding to the stack of computer paper on his desk.

"That's just it. I don't know her name."

Tabitha put her hands on her hips. "Then how do you expect to find her?"

"Looking at this list, I'm not sure I will."

"Well, good luck. And if you need any more help, just let me know," she said with a cheerful wave before shutting the door on her way out.

Michael was tempted to ask her assistance in his search for Cassie, but he figured the less he said about the artist, the more unlikely it was anyone would discover he'd met her at the dating service dinner. It wouldn't be so bad if he hadn't made such a fuss about being an unwilling participant, telling Tabitha he only attended the dinner because he hadn't wanted to hurt Tessie.

His assistant had asked him about his evening out the following Monday morning. She'd listened intently as he'd given as brief an explanation as was possible, saying that although it wasn't as bad as he'd expected, it wasn't the way he wanted to meet women. Then he'd waited a couple of days before asking about the art galleries, not wanting Tabitha to question why he suddenly had an interest in art.

He didn't. He'd always been a science guy, needing things to be concrete, not abstract. Which was why it was probably foolish of him to be entertaining thoughts that he and this Cassie could enjoy more than a couple of glasses of wine and some titillating conversation.

But he did entertain such thoughts. Ever since the dinner, she'd been on his mind often—which really had him perplexed. He wasn't one to fall head over heels for a woman at the first meeting—certainly it had never happened to him before. Maybe his fascination with her had to do with the fact that Cassie wanted nothing to do with him. Maybe if she hadn't told Claudia Dixon to blow him off, he wouldn't now, six days later, be trying to figure out how to find her.

But he *was* trying to locate her. That's why he'd had Tabitha go on the Internet and get a listing of the local art galleries. He hoped to find a Cassie among the names, but when he'd read through all of the pages without any success, he decided it was like trying to find a needle in a haystack.

For all he knew, she might have been a starving artist—and a not very good one at that. Maybe she'd never shown her work. Or maybe she only talked about being an artist but hadn't actually created a single work of art. He threw the computer printout into a desk drawer.

He needed to forget about Cassie the artist. Meeting a woman through a dating service was not his idea of romance anyway. And he didn't want his mother to get any more ideas on the subject, which meant there was something he had to do. He unlocked the center drawer on his desk and pulled it open. The only item inside was a black book.

He picked it up and flipped through the alphabet until he came to the 'T' section. When Rebecca Tollefson dated a guy, she made sure everyone around knew he was her possession. The thought made him shiver. Still he picked up the phone and dialed her number.

"Rebecca, Mac."

After a throaty chuckle of delight, which conjured up all sorts of provocative images in his mind, she said, "I'm so glad you called. I thought you'd forgotten about me."

"Now how could I do that? You've been on my mind a lot lately and I was wondering, are you free on Sunday?"

AFTER A BUSY WEEK at the clinic that had included several emergencies, which had robbed him of sleep on three out of the past six nights, Michael was not in the best of moods on Sunday when he picked up Rebecca. It didn't help that she wanted to spend the day in the city and would have been perfectly content not to leave his place.

The city was not where he wanted to spend his afternoon. Ever since he'd graduated from college he'd lived alone in a condominium the real estate agent had called the perfect residence for the young professional. It was in a high-rise that gave him a spectacular view of the metropolitan area and easy access to the clinic and its patients. It also had its own health club, tennis courts and swimming pool.

Rebecca saw no reason to leave the complex when they had everything they needed at their fingertips. Not even when Michael told her that he wanted to take her to the lake so that she could meet his mother did she change her mind. It was only after much cajoling and the promise that they would later return to the nightclub just around the corner that she agreed to spend the afternoon at Tessie's.

As he pulled into the long, winding driveway leading to the house, Rebecca said, "This is quaint, isn't it?"

Michael didn't comment, but hoped that when she stepped inside the house she wouldn't remark on how old the house was. It wasn't the fanciest of houses, but it was the one he'd called home ever since he could remember. He loved its high ceilings and varnished wood floors. He also knew that no matter what day of the week or what time of day it was, Tessie would welcome him with open arms. Whether she would welcome Rebecca was anyone's guess.

Although he didn't like the idea of allowing his mother to believe that Rebecca was anything other than a woman he occasionally dated, he knew that if he was going to get Tessie to stop her matchmaking, he needed to convince her that he was getting serious about Rebecca. Only he soon discovered that Tessie was nowhere in sight.

Rebecca could only pierce him with one of her "I told you I didn't want to come" stares and said, "Guess you should have called first."

"She's always home on Sundays," he said, walking around to the side of the house, where he peeked

into a small window in the garage. "Her car's here."
He followed the sidewalk to the back of the house.
She wasn't in the garden, nor sitting on the patio, nor
rocking in her wicker chair in the gazebo.

"You looking for Tessie?"

Michael glanced across the honeysuckle hedge to
see Otto, the next-door neighbor and husband to one
of the Mums, sprinkling his garden. "Have you seen
her today?" he asked the balding gentleman.

"Sure did. She took off with a couple of the Mums
right after church. Nan said they were going to the
senior citizen center. Apparently they have some big
doings going on over there, but Nan and I couldn't
go. We're baby-sitting the grandkids."

"Thanks." Michael acknowledged the information
with a wave of his hand, then turned to Rebecca, who
stood tapping her foot near the Explorer. She'd heard
every word of his conversation with Otto so he didn't
have to repeat it.

"Does that mean we can leave?" she asked, im-
patience twisting her lovely features into a scowl.

He hadn't put up with Rebecca for this long to give
up on his plan because of a little detour. "If I know
Tessie, she won't stay away very long on a beautiful
day like this."

"You want to wait for her to come home?"

It was obvious that Rebecca didn't. "It's not as if
there isn't anything to do," he said with as charming
a smile as he could muster. He nodded to her small
designer cloth bag. "Put your suit on and we'll go
for a swim."

She wrinkled her nose. "In the lake?"

"Sure, why not?"

"Because it's dirty, for one thing."

"It's perfectly safe for swimming, if that's what's worrying you."

"The last time I swam in a lake I cut my foot on a rusty beer can."

"This is private property and I know for a fact that Tessie doesn't drink beer."

"But what about the creepy crawly things...oh, and those slimy black leeches?" She practically shivered at the thought. "And the bottom's probably full of yuck."

"There are a few weeds, but all the home owners in this bay have the beach raked for weeds every summer." She didn't look convinced so he said, "What about going for a boat ride?"

"I suppose I can do that," she told him, although judging by the slight pout to her lips, she wasn't thrilled with that suggestion, either.

"You want to change into your swimsuit first?" he asked.

She glanced around nervously. "Out here?"

"No, in the house. I have a key." He realized then that, although Rebecca came in a pretty package, she wasn't exactly the sharpest knife in the drawer.

She shrugged. "I suppose I should. Then I can put my hair up, too, so the wind doesn't destroy the curl. You wouldn't want me looking like a witch when we go out tonight, would you?"

Actually, he didn't care how she looked, for he was wishing he hadn't asked her out at all. Other than her stunning good looks, he found nothing attractive about her and was relieved when his pager buzzed. "I'm being paged," he said, reaching for the slim device in his pocket.

"Don't you ever turn that thing off?"

"Can't. I'm on call."

"But it's your day off."

"Yes, but that doesn't mean emergencies can't happen." He glanced at the number and saw that it wasn't the clinic's answering service. He walked back to the Explorer to use the cell phone.

He punched in the seven numbers and was surprised to hear Tessie's voice. "Michael? Is that you?"

"Yes, Mom. Where are you?"

"I'm at the senior citizen center, dear. They had the most wonderful chicken dinner. I'm sorry I didn't ask you to join us. I know how much you like chicken."

"It's okay, Mom. I had other plans for today."

"Oh, I'm getting you away from something important, aren't I?" she fretted.

"No, you're not. It's my day off and you're going to be surprised to hear this, but I'm at the lake. I brought a friend over I wanted you to meet."

"And now I'm not there! Oh Michael, I wished you had called me!"

"It's all right. We'll stay here until you get home."

"But that's the problem. I don't know when I'm going to get home. Louella's car died."

"It won't start?"

"When she turns the key, nothing happens. It just makes this clicking sound."

"Starter's probably gone," he guessed.

"Oh my, that sounds serious. Do you think she should call the service station and have a tow truck come out?"

"That's not necessary, I'll come there and check it out."

He could hear her say in an aside, "He's going to come look at it."

He heard a second voice in the background say, "Oh, he's such a dear boy. Are you sure we're not interrupting his plans?"

"Michael, Louella appreciates your offer, but she doesn't want to impose on your time. She knows you've been working long hours at the clinic and if you've finally found a lady friend..."

He glanced at Rebecca, who sat on the lawn swing in the shade of an elm tree looking extremely bored. Suddenly he was having second thoughts about introducing her to Tessie.

"I didn't say it was a lady."

"Is it?"

He didn't answer but said, "Tell Louella I'll come see what I can do. If nothing else, I can give you and the others a ride home while she has the car towed to the station."

"That's so sweet of you. Where should we wait for you? Outside the front doors?"

Michael frowned. The temperature had climbed well into the eighties. Standing on a concrete sidewalk with the sun beating down on them wouldn't be wise for the senior ladies. "Stay inside in the air-conditioning, Mom. I'll find you."

"All right, dear. You know where the center is, don't you? It's just a couple of blocks off Main Street."

"I know where it is." He glanced at his watch. "It might take me a little longer than usual because I have something to do first, but I'll be there. Okay?"

"All right. And Michael, bring your lady friend. I want to meet her," Tessie said, then hung up.

After the way the afternoon had gone, he knew it would be a mistake to take Rebecca to the senior citizen center. As much as he hated driving all the way into the city and then back to the Minnetonka area again, he knew he really didn't have much choice.

"Don't tell me. You have an emergency," she said as he walked back over to where she sat on the lawn swing.

"I'm afraid my services are needed," he told her. It wasn't a lie. Tessie did need him.

Rebecca rolled her eyes. "I should have known. It's always like this, isn't it?" She didn't let him answer before she added, "You should add more staff to that clinic of yours."

He didn't answer but said, "Come. I'll take you home."

"Is it going to take all day, this emergency?" she asked as he held the door open for her. "Maybe we can still meet for drinks this evening?"

"I'd like to, but I'm not sure how long this will take. There'll be other hot summer nights," he said with a promising smile, although he knew there wouldn't be.

As soon as they'd parted company, he felt relieved that Tessie hadn't been home this afternoon. It would have been a mistake to mislead her into thinking that he had something going with Rebecca.

WHEN HE ARRIVED at the senior citizen center, his mother and three of the Mums were waiting for him outside the front doors of the building. He pulled up in the no-loading zone and climbed out.

"Where's your friend?" Tessie asked as he walked over to them.

"There was a change in plans. You should be inside where it's cool," he said, noticing that despite the awning shadowing the front walk, the air was hot and close.

"We were until just a minute ago, but then the man from the service station came to tow Louella's truck and she had to give him the keys, so we came outside with her." The other three Mums bobbed their heads in agreement.

Michael shoved his hands to his waist. "I thought you were going to wait for me to take a look at Louella's car before you called the station?"

It was Louella who answered. "I have an automobile club card. Towing's included in my membership."

"Would you like to come inside, Michael, and see the pictures Emmet put up in the recreation room?" Tessie asked.

Before he could answer, Violet said, "He probably doesn't want to look at a bunch of old people."

Tessie clicked her tongue. "Of course, he would. They're wonderful pictures."

"Don't pay any attention to her," Agnes, the fourth Mum told him. "She's just saying that because she wants to get home in time to watch the garden show on cable."

"If Michael wants to go inside and see the pictures, he can go inside," Violet insisted. "I'm not in a hurry."

Michael suspected from the way she clutched her bag that she couldn't get out of there fast enough.

"It's all right, Vi. I can come back another time and see them."

"They're going to be here for the whole month of June," Louella pointed out.

"I'd like another look myself," Tessie told him. "Maybe you and I can come next weekend?" She looked up at him with a hopeful look in her eyes.

"Sure," he answered. "Is everybody ready to leave then?"

After a chorus of yeses, he led them over to the Explorer parked at the curb and drove each of them home.

It was a few hours later, when Michael had parked his vehicle in the underground garage at his complex, that he noticed one of the ladies had left something on the seat behind him. A sheer blue scarf covered a pink booklet, which upon closer inspection turned out to be a guide to the portraits on display at the senior citizen center.

"'Everlasting Love. A look at marriage in the golden years,'" he read aloud. So these were the pictures Tessie had wanted him to see. He smiled. Always the romantic, she'd wanted to show him the couples whose love had lasted more than half a century.

He doubted anyone would miss the brochure, but he guessed that whoever owned the scarf would be looking for it and wondering where she'd left it.

Before he'd even unlocked the door to his condominium, he could hear the phone ringing. As soon as he was inside, he made a dash for the cordless lying on the end table beside his sofa.

It was Tessie. "Oh good. You're finally home."

"I bet you're calling about the scarf," he said, tossing it and the brochure onto the coffee table.

"You found it?"

"On the backseat. Is it Violet's?"

"No, it's Louella's. She also left the program, which is what she was really worried about. She didn't want you to think it wasn't important and toss it out."

"I wouldn't throw anything away without asking you first," he assured her.

"I know that. She was concerned because her cousin is number seventeen in the exhibit, so of course she wants to keep the program as a souvenir," Tessie told him.

"Of course," he answered, plopping down onto the sofa. He leaned back and was about to close his eyes when he noticed a picture on the back of the pink brochure. Through the sheer blue fabric of the scarf it was blurred, but there was something familiar about the face staring up at him.

He pulled the brochure out from beneath the scarf and saw the reason why. It was Cassie, the artist, the woman he'd sat next to at the dating service dinner. He read the small print next to the photograph.

"Artist Cassandra Carrigan's own grandparents were the inspiration for her 'Everlasting Love' exhibit. For more information about Ms. Carrigan's work, you can contact her at…"

A splotch of coffee or something liquid had smudged the telephone number printed on the brochure. Michael frowned.

"Michael, are you there?"

He realized he hadn't been listening to his mother.

"Yeah, I'm here. Mom, about this art exhibit at the center, was the artist there today?"

"No, I wish she had been. I would have liked to congratulate her personally. Emmet told me she was there last night. They had an opening celebration, but it was Louella's granddaughter's music recital and the Mums wanted to go and show her our support."

"So Emmet knows her?"

"Why, yes. He arranged for the art to be shown at the center, and he and his wife Dorothy are in one of the pictures. I wish you had come inside to see the portraits. They are so beautiful. Emmet says we're very lucky she chose the center to display her work. Someday she's going to be famous."

Michael flipped through the pages looking for more information on the artist, but there was none, only a brief description of each of the portraits in the exhibit. He turned again to the photograph on the back page.

Smiling at him the same way she'd smiled at him during dinner was Cassie the artist. A shiver of excitement traveled through him. Just when he thought he'd never see her again, he'd found her.

"Michael, did you hear me? I said someday she's going to be famous."

He smiled broadly. "I think you might just be right." And if he had anything to say about it, his mother would get her wish to meet the artist. Soon.

Chapter Four

As soon as Michael got off the phone, he pulled out the Minneapolis and St. Paul phone books. There was no Cassandra Carrigan listed in either one. Nor was there a listing for her with directory assistance. She either had an unlisted number or she didn't live in the Twin Cities.

He knew the latter was a possibility. Just because she had used a Twin City dating service didn't necessarily mean that she lived in the metropolitan area. She could be from any one of the numerous small towns on the outskirts of the cities.

He looked again at the tiny photo on the back of the pink brochure. There was something intriguing about the way she smiled into the camera. It reminded him of the way she'd looked at him at the dating service dinner. Just thinking about her stirred something inside him.

He wanted to see this woman again. And he had a pretty good idea that she would welcome his attention—despite what Claudia Dixon had said. There was only one thing to do. He reached for the phone and dialed Tessie's number.

"Mom, how about if I drop Violet's scarf off tomorrow? Then you and I can go over to the senior citizen center and see the art exhibit. From what this brochure say, it sounds like something I'm going to enjoy.''

"DIDN'T I TELL YOU they were beautiful?'' Tessie asked Michael as he studied a portrait of a couple gazing at each other with obvious devotion.

"Yes, they are,'' Michael agreed, surprised by the emotion the artist had managed to capture in each picture. The personality of the individuals had come through with a startling clarity. The longer he stared at the portraits, the more intrigued he became with the artist.

He wondered why she didn't use Cassie as her professional name, unless she preferred to keep her personal life separate from her professional one. By the time he'd seen the entire exhibit, he was no closer to finding out who she was than he'd been yesterday at this time. The programs were gone and except for a small "About the Artist'' posted near the door, there was no information on Cassandra Carrigan.

"I wonder if she has anything for sale,'' he commented as his mother admired the last of the portraits.

"Doesn't it say in the program?''

He spread his empty hands. "Couldn't find one. Apparently they're out.''

"Oh, that's a shame. I suppose we could ask Emmet. He's the one who arranged for her to do all of this,'' she said with a wave of her hand.

"Is he working tonight?'' Michael asked as they stepped out into the corridor.

"If he is, he'll be in the office. Ooh—I see a friend of mine.'' She waved at an elderly woman at the opposite end of the hall. "Maybe we ought to have a cup of coffee in the beverage center."

"I'll tell you what. You go say hello to your friend and I'll go see if I can find Mr. Sandberg. Then we'll meet for coffee, okay?"

"You know where the beverage center is?" she asked, concern lining her brow.

"I'm sure I can find it," he told her with an indulgent smile, relieved that he had an excuse not to have his mother present when he inquired about Cassandra Carrigan.

As soon as she had disappeared down the corridor, he walked back toward the front entrance to the director's office. "Mr. Sandberg, I'm Michael McFerrin."

"Ah, Dr. Mac. I've heard a lot about you. It's good to finally meet you," the silver-haired gentleman said, rising to his feet to shake his hand.

"I feel the same way. I've heard a lot of good things about the center and I'm very impressed by the art exhibit."

"Isn't it something?" He gestured for Michael to take a seat. "Folks from the paper were here yesterday. There's going to be a big article in next Sunday's Arts and Entertainment section and rightly so. What that lady can do with a bunch of colored chalk." He shook his head in amazement.

"She definitely has talent. Tessie said you know her?" he asked, his heart pumping faster at the thought that he was finally going to get somewhere in his quest to find Cassie.

"Yes, and I can tell you she is one special lady."

"Sounds as if you like her."

"What's not to like? She's beautiful, she's smart,

she's young and she's talented.'' He spread his arms expressively. ''Just look at what she's done. How many people do you who know would spend two years working on portraits of old people?''

''It's a wonderful exhibit. Are any of the portraits for sale?''

He shook his head. ''I'm afraid not. They went very fast, as you can well imagine. And if you ask me, she didn't charge nearly enough money for them. She wouldn't have taken anything for the one she did of me and my wife, but I put my foot down and told her she had to take something.''

''So she's not making much of a profit from them?'' he repeated, making sure he understood.

''No, sir. I think she knows most of the seniors are on fixed incomes and she wanted to make them affordable.''

Michael nodded his head in understanding. ''Maybe art is a hobby for her.''

''Dorothy did say she has another job, but I say if she's not doing pictures like that for a living, it's a real shame. She is about the sweetest young thing I've ever met. And very pretty, too.'' He smiled, wiggling brows in a gesture every man understood.

''And is there a Mr. Carrigan?''

''A husband? No.'' The smile slid from his face. ''She's a widow. Apparently her husband was an actor who was just starting to make it big when he was killed in some kind of accident where he worked. The really sad part is that she's never gotten over him. I guess she'd rather be single the rest of her life—at least that's what she told Dorothy.''

Obviously Dorothy was unaware that Cassandra Carrigan belonged to a dating service. That was a puzzle piece Michael didn't understand. He agreed with Emmet Sandberg. She was beautiful, smart and talented. So what was she doing at Dinner Date?

"Were you interested in buying one of the portraits?" Emmet asked.

Michael nodded. "Or some of her other work, if she has pieces for sale. Is there a way I can contact her?"

"Her studio number is on the program," Emmet answered.

"I didn't see any in the recreation hall."

"That's because the exhibit was more popular than we anticipated and we ran out, but I think I have a few of them left on my desk." He shuffled through a pile of papers until he found the pink brochure. "Yes. Here it is." He handed the program to Michael, who gazed at it with a sense of accomplishment.

Finally he had Cassie's phone number in his hands. Michael couldn't have hid his smile had he wanted to.

"Thank you. I just might give her a call and see what she has. I've never been one to collect art, but then I've never seen anything like those portraits before. They're just…" He paused dramatically, as if searching for the right words to convey his emotion.

"I know what you mean," Emmet finished for him. "I feel the same way when I look at them."

Michael rose to leave. "It's a great exhibit. You are to be complimented, Mr. Sandberg. And I appreciate your help with this." He tapped the brochure against the palm of his hand.

"You don't need to thank me. I'm only doing my job." He came around the desk to walk Michael to the door. "I'm glad I could be of assistance. I only hope Cassandra has what you're looking for."

"Oh, I think she does," he said confidently. "I think she does."

CASSIE LOOKED AT THE CLOCK and sighed. She'd been working at her computer for nearly four hours and she still hadn't come up with a suitable design for the technical illustration requested by her client.

It shouldn't have surprised her. Creating designs on a computer was not how she wanted to be doing graphic illustration, yet the job market dictated the medium, and if she was going to pay her bills, she needed to give clients what they wanted. Right now this client wanted a computer-generated illustration.

As if understanding her need to be distracted, Degas, her Abyssinian cat, jumped up on her workstation. Wrapped around one paw was pink yarn with a small crocheted ball at the end, which tinkled as Degas batted it about.

"As much as I'd rather be playing with you, I can't," she told her pet, lifting him and depositing him back on the floor. "If I don't finish this today, there will be no tuna in your bowl tomorrow."

The Abyssinian gave a haughty meow, as if sassing his master.

"No," Cassie repeated.

Then came the look—the one intended to make Cassie feel as if Degas were neglected and needed to have his ears scratched. Fortunately the phone rang and she had an excuse to turn her back on that look. As she reached for the cordless, Degas leaped up next to it and meowed, as if reminding her she didn't answer the phone during working hours.

Cassie waited for the answering machine to kick in, then listened to see who was calling before picking up the receiver. Cat or no cat, if she wanted to talk on the phone, she would.

The voice on the other end, however, was not someone she knew, although something in the deep, masculine tone sounded familiar.

"I'm calling for Cassandra Carrigan. I saw the portrait exhibit at the senior citizen center and would like to talk to her about other pieces she might have for sale. If she would get back to me as soon as possible, I'd appreciate it. I can be reached at the following number."

Cassie reached for a Post-it and jotted down the number before the machine beeped. She replayed the message, thinking she must have missed the man's name. She hadn't. He hadn't given his name, only a number. She wrote "possible sale" at the top of the phone message and stuck it next to the half-dozen other messages she'd received that day. Until she finished her job for the engineering firm, she wasn't going to look at any of them.

Only the message from the man with no name intrigued her. The voice had sounded strangely familiar. She racked her brain trying to think where she may have heard it before. Not more than a half hour had gone by when she reached for the piece of paper and dialed the number. It wasn't a direct connection, but an electronic answering system indicating she had reached a pager. She punched in her number followed by the pound sign, then hung up and waited for the return call.

It didn't take long. Within only a couple of minutes

the phone rang. This time she didn't hesitate to pick
it up.

"This is Cassandra."

"Hello, Cassandra." As she expected, it was a man
with a faintly familiar voice that was low and husky
so that the way he said her name made her feel as if
someone were pulling velvet across her bare flesh. "I
called you about the art."

"Yes, Mr…?"

"McFerrin."

McFerrin. She ran the name through her memory
bank, but didn't come up with a face to match it. Must
have been her imagination that his voice sounded
vaguely familiar.

"Yes, Mr. McFerrin. How may I help you?"

"I saw the exhibit at the senior citizen center and
I was hoping I could buy one of your pieces, but
Emmet Sandberg said they weren't for sale."

"That's right, they're not."

"I'm disappointed. Your use of pastels is incredible."

The compliment sent a tiny shiver of pleasure
through her—or was it the timbre of his voice?
"Thank you."

"I'd like to see more of your work."

She glanced across her studio to where a half-dozen
framed pastels were propped against the wall. All of
them were children she'd sketched while sitting in the
park. Although she'd finished them months ago, she
hadn't been able to part with any of them.

"I'm fairly new to the art world, Mr. McFerrin.
'Everlasting Love' is my first show."

"Then you don't have other pastels for sale," he
said on a note of disappointment.

"Not at this time, no," she answered, feeling a twinge of guilt at the portraits staring at her from across the room.

He sighed. "I'm disappointed. I'd hoped to purchase one as a gift." He paused, then said, "What about commissioned work?"

The question caught her off guard. Friends and family members often requested she do portraits for them, but never had a complete stranger approached her with the request. "You want to hire me to sketch someone's portrait?"

"Yes, if we can come to acceptable terms."

Cassie's excitement ebbed. There was the catch. The terms. Her limited experience in the art world had shown her that few people understood the number of hours that went into portrait work.

"Mr. McFerrin, do you have any idea what a portrait like the ones at the senior citizen center are worth?"

"No, but the person I want sketched is priceless to me." He went on to quote a figure that indicated he was indeed very aware of what it cost to commission a portrait artist.

Not that Cassie had established her reputation in the field. "As I said, I'm still earning my reputation, but I would be happy to meet with you to discuss what your expectations are and then I can tell you if I'm the right artist for your project."

"That would be great."

She glanced at her calendar. "Are we looking at daytime or evening?"

"Actually, the only time I'm free is Saturday evening."

"Unfortunately I work Saturday evenings," she

told him, mentally debating whether she should call Claudia and tell her she'd have to pass on this week's Dinner Date.

"What about next Saturday?" he asked.

"That's not good, either. There is no other day that would work for you?"

"I wish I could say there was, but there just isn't." He sighed. "And I was so hoping we could get together on this."

So was Cassie. The amount of money a private commission would bring in would make her income from the dating service look like peanuts. "What about if we met at four o'clock on Saturday?"

He paused, as if looking at his schedule, then said, "No, it looks like the earliest I'm free is seven."

Cassie hesitated. She hated backing out on Claudia after she'd said she would work, but she also knew that her best friend would understand that an opportunity like this was one she couldn't pass up.

"I can probably rework my schedule to make it at seven," she told him.

"Great. I'll take you to dinner."

That had Cassie squirming. If she had dinner with this man, there'd be that awkwardness regarding who would pay. He the client, or she the one selling her services? Yet she didn't want him coming to her studio. She supposed she could always call Emmet Sandberg to find out more about him. Thinking about the director of the senior citizen center gave her an idea.

"I'm afraid I must say no to dinner, but we can have coffee. Maybe we should meet at the senior citizen center?" she suggested. "After all, that's where most of my portraits are at the moment and we both know where it's located. Seven okay with you?"

There was a long pause and she thought she detected a sigh of frustration. Then he said, "Seven will be fine."

"All right. I'll meet you at the entrance to the exhibit. I'm a blonde, about five-five—"

"I know what you look like, Ms. Carrigan."

That gave her a moment of concern and she was silent.

"Your picture's on the program at the center."

"Oh, that's right. What about you? I don't know what you look like," she said.

"Don't worry. I'm sure we'll have no problem connecting."

ALTHOUGH CASSIE KNEW that not every group Claudia put together had a facilitator from the dating service, it bothered her to have to ask her friend for time off. Once she had given her word, she seldom changed it. As she expected, Claudia understood why she couldn't be at the Dinner Date assignment on Saturday night.

Getting a portrait commission had been her goal and to get paid the kind of money Mr. McFerrin was willing to give her made the evening an important one to her career. Claudia agreed, which was why she helped Cassie draft a written contract pertaining to the commissioned work. It was inside her briefcase that sat beside her on the front seat of her car.

Cassie was grateful that her best friend had a business head, because she certainly didn't possess one. It was the reason she'd be a starving artist if she didn't have a second job. Cassie found it difficult to put a price tag on her work and oftentimes ended up giving it away, much to Claudia's dismay.

But not tonight. She and Claudia had already cal-
culated the approximate number of hours it would
take to do a portrait and the cost of the materials she
needed to buy. When Mr. McFerrin sat down to do
business with her, she would be negotiating as a professional, not as a starving artist.

She didn't like discussing money, and especially
not when it came to her work. As she pulled into the
parking lot of the senior citizen center, anxiety left a
trail of indigestion blazing through her chest. What
she needed was a roll of antacids. The car's clock
said 6:37, which meant she had time to make a quick
dash to the convenience store across the street from
the center.

After parking her car, she walked the short distance
to the Quick Stop. As she walked past the fuel islands
she noticed a man pumping gas into an Explorer. He
was tall, dark and handsome, and very familiar looking. Cassie's heart fluttered as she realized why she
recognized him.

It was Dr. Mac, one of the guests at a Dinner Date
engagement she'd worked two weeks ago. In the six
months Cassie had worked for the dating service,
never had she run into any of its clients when she
hadn't been working. Claudia had told her that in a
metropolitan area the size of the Twin Cities, it would
be unusual if she were to see someone from one of
the dinners.

Here she was, far from the downtown area where
Dinner Date scheduled their gatherings, yet she was
less than thirty feet from one of Claudia's clients. A
client who'd been rather persistent in his attempts to
get Cassie's phone number. If chance had to put one
of the single men from the dating service in her path,

why did it have to be one who'd shown an interest in her?

Cassie knew if she didn't do something quickly, he'd see her and she'd be even more uncomfortable. Instead of going into the convenience store, she made a beeline for the video rental outlet next door. She went straight to the children's section, which was located in the front of store behind the plate glass windows. From where she stood she could see outside to the parking lot, yet she could duck behind the tall shelves if necessary.

Pretending to read the package of a recent release, she glanced outside to the fuel pumps. Dr. Mac's shoulders were broad, his arms thick with muscles as he washed his windows, then wiped them dry with paper towels. He wore a dark blue knit shirt tucked inside a pair of tan slacks. As a redheaded woman pulled up to the pump across from him, Cassie noticed he eyed her curiously. Typical male, she thought.

When the woman dropped her keys on the pavement, he was quick to reach across and pick them up for her. The smile he gave the redhead sent a tingling through Cassie as she remembered him smiling at her in the same way. The redhead must have said something clever or funny, for Dr. Mac laughed.

Then he disappeared inside the store. When he came back outside, Cassie thought he might say something to the redhead, but he didn't. He simply got in his Explorer and drove away. From where she stood, it was impossible to see in which direction he went.

When she was certain he was out of sight, she put the children's video back on the shelf and headed for the convenience store. She bought a package of antacids, which she opened immediately, popped one into her mouth and headed back to the senior citizen center.

By the time she stepped into the air-conditioned building, she was feeling much more relaxed about the meeting ahead of her. Nothing like a little distraction to take the edge off a business appointment, she thought as she freshened up in the women's rest room. When she'd combed her hair and smoothed on another coat of Barely There lipstick, she hoisted her portfolio under one arm and her briefcase in the other, then made her way to the art exhibit.

As usual, whenever she saw her work on display, she felt a quiver of pride. Emmet Sandberg had told her he'd received dozens of calls requesting information on the portraits, but until the newspaper reporter had interviewed her, she'd assumed the interest was due to the age of her models. A glance inside the recreation room told her it wasn't simply the retired community that found her work interesting.

So engrossed was she in watching others look at her portraits that she didn't hear anyone approach and was startled when a man's voice said, "So we meet again, Cassie the artist."

She spun around and saw Dr. Mac, the man who only a short time earlier she'd done her best to avoid. He was there, in her face, and looking very pleased that he'd found her. She couldn't help but notice how tall he was. Sitting down at the dinner table, she hadn't realized what a commanding figure he was on his feet and she'd forgotten how dazzling his smile could be. He was good-looking—so good-looking Cassie went a little dry in the mouth. It didn't help that he was smiling at her as if she were the only thing of interest in the entire universe.

"Hello, Dr. Mac," she finally managed to say, trying not to let him see how rattled she was by his appearance. She didn't want to smile at him, but she couldn't help herself. He had an infectious grin.

"Actually, it's Dr. McFerrin," he said with a bit of mischief in his eyes.

A chill chased away any warmth she may have been feeling toward him. "*You're* Mr. McFerrin?"

"Michael McFerrin," he said, extending his hand to her.

She felt as if she'd been duped. From the minute he'd seen her picture on the art program he'd known who she was, yet when he'd called he'd led her to believe he was a complete stranger interested in buying her art.

"Why didn't you tell me who you were when you called?" she asked, ignoring his outstretched hand.

"And would you have agreed to meet me?"

"No. Dinner Date promises anonymity. *This*—" she wiggled her finger between the two of them "—is not anonymity."

"So you won't do business with me because we happened to be at the same dinner?"

"That's why you're here? To do business?" Skepticism lifted one brow.

"And what other reason would there be? You made it perfectly clear to Claudia Dixon that you didn't want to have anything to do with Dr. Mac, the veterinarian," he reminded her, all warmth gone from his face.

She couldn't help but blush. "You're making this very awkward."

"Does that mean you don't want to do business?"

Of course she did, but not with this man. She was tempted to say no, but then she could only imagine what Claudia would say if she learned that Cassie had turned down commissioned work because she was embarrassed.

"Business is why I'm here." She didn't mean for it to sound so cutting, but it did.

"Then why don't we start over. Let's forget about the dinner at the supper club." Again he extended his hand. "I'm Michael McFerrin."

"Cassandra Carrigan." She reluctantly placed her hand in his and hated the tingling it created in her body. She didn't want to feel anything for him and quickly removed it from his grasp.

"Should we go to the cafeteria and discuss the portrait?" he asked.

"I talked to Emmet Sandberg and he said we could use one of the conference rooms. It's just around the corner." She reached for her portfolio, but he had already lifted the cumbersome leather case. She put her hands on the strap and gently eased it from him. "I prefer to carry this myself."

He lifted his brows and asked, "What about the briefcase? Am I allowed to help you with that?"

For an answer, she picked up the leather briefcase with her other hand. If anyone had any doubt there was tension between them, their body language said it all. They looked like two people ready to square off in Judge Judy's courtroom instead of about to do business together.

At the conference room he held the door open for her and she murmured a polite thank-you. There were several long tables, which she used to display her art.

Without saying a word, she pulled the pieces from her portfolio, all the time aware of his eyes on her.

"I thought I should bring you some of the work I've done using younger models," she said as she set the portraits she'd done at the playground on the table. "You didn't mention the age of the person you want me to sketch."

Seeing the children's faces softened his stiff demeanor. "Do you know these kids?"

"I didn't when I first sketched them, but then I spent so much time at the park watching them I thought it would be wise to introduce myself to their mothers. I know if I were a mother I wouldn't want some stranger watching my kids so closely."

"You don't have children?"

"No."

He scrutinized each portrait with great patience. "You put so much life into faces. You have a rare gift."

She could see that it was a genuine compliment and it warmed her. "Thank you." He continued to examine each of the pastels. Wondering what thoughts were going through his head as he silently studied each one, she said, "As you can see, I'm very traditional in my work whatever the age of the subject."

"How long does it take it to do something like this from start to finish?"

"It varies. Some take longer than others." She didn't want to tell him that one of the variables was how much moonlighting she had to do. Although she called herself a portrait artist by profession, until now it hadn't paid her bills.

"Do you do much commissioned work?"

"Some," she answered evasively.

"Would the person you're sketching have to sit for long periods of time?"

"Again, it depends on the model. I usually do a pencil sketch of the pose I want to use and take some photographs to cut down on the amount of time the subject must sit."

He appeared relieved by her answer. "That would probably work then."

"Would work for what, Mr. McFerrin?"

"My mother. She's eighty-one and about as active as a twenty-year-old. I don't know if I could get her to sit still very long." Again there was that infectious grin.

Cassie had to use every muscle she possessed not to respond to it. "She wouldn't have to sit for long periods of time," she told him coolly, relieved that the subject he had in mind was an older woman, not a younger one. Her experience had been that the seniors were much easier to satisfy than the younger generation.

"Where is your studio?"

"Near the Uptown area of Minneapolis."

He frowned. "That could be a problem. My mother lives on Lake Minnetonka. Would you be willing to sketch her in her home?"

"I did most of the seniors in the exhibit in their homes," she told him, "But..." She trailed off, wondering if the reason he wanted his mother sketched in her home was because he still lived with her and hoped to see her there.

"But what, Ms. Carrigan?"

"Does your mother drive?"

He smiled. "Oh, yes, but I'd rather she didn't at times. She's had several small fender benders in the past year and all of them occurred in the city. I trust her to get to the grocery store and to see her friends out here by the lake, but the city…well, that's another story.''

She nodded in understanding.

"So, do we have a deal?'' he asked.

"We haven't talked terms," she reminded him, flipping open her briefcase. She pulled out the agreement Claudia had drafted and handed it to him. "This is my standard contract. If you want to take it home and look at, you can call me when you've made your decision.'' She tried to sound very professional. "If you choose to have me do your mother's portrait, we'll set up an appointment and get started.''

"I don't need to take it home and look at it, Ms. Carrigan. I know what I want.''

Cassie had the feeling that he wasn't only referring to her art. She took a deep breath and said, "Mr. McFerrin, I think we need to get something straight here.''

He spread his hands. "Be my guest. Say whatever it is you have to say.''

"You contacted me as Cassandra Carrigan, the artist, not as Cassie the woman you met through Dinner Date," she said stiffly. "If we see each other again, it's business. Nothing else.''

If a smile could make him charming, a frown could make him very intimidating. His face lost all traces of any warmth as he said, "You've made yourself perfectly clear, Ms. Carrigan. I want a portrait of my mother. I don't want you.''

Cassie shivered and wished she hadn't said anything. But it was over and done with now. She'd paint his mother, get paid and never have to see him again.

Chapter Five

All the way home from his appointment with Cassandra Carrigan, Michael repeatedly asked himself the same question. What had happened to Cassie the artist—the warm, vibrant woman who had charmed every man at the Dinner Date gathering?

If it wasn't for the fact that she was an incredible artist and he wanted a pastel portrait of Tessie, Michael would have been out of the senior citizen center the minute Cassie had given him the haughty look that had said, "Don't even think about being interested in me as a woman because I want nothing to do with you."

He could hardly believe it was the same woman who'd looked at him at the restaurant as if he were Brad Pitt. Gone was the flirtatious sparkle that had invited his attention. He wondered how she could have been so incredibly charismatic one night and so obtusely difficult another. Had it all been an act at dinner? Or was she simply a tease—a woman who enjoyed leading men on and then slapping them down with a pointed look of disgust?

At least now he understood why Claudia Dixon had refused his request to arrange dinner for the two of them. He had a pretty good idea that the dating service director knew the artist well. Hell, Cassie was probably one of her best-paying customers. A fickle woman who kept coming back for another chance at meeting Mr. Right. Enough Cassandra Carrigans and Claudia Dixon could be a wealthy woman.

He made a sarcastic sound. He'd seen enough fickle women in his lifetime to know that he wanted to steer clear of this particular one—whether she was beautiful or not.

And Cassie was beautiful. That blond hair, those perfectly shaped lips covered with only a hint of pink. She may have been every dating service director's dream client, but she was a man's worst nightmare. She didn't know what she wanted, and even when she thought she had it figured out, she'd change her mind.

He could only shake his head in regret. At least he'd found out what kind of a woman Cassie Carrigan was before he'd made an even bigger fool of himself. In thirty-five years he hadn't forced his attention on any woman and he wasn't planning to start now. If she thought he was going to be hanging around, hoping to get a glimpse of her, she was wrong. He didn't care if he ever saw her again.

If it wasn't for the fact that Tessie's cottage was a difficult place to find—even with the best of directions—he wouldn't have had to see her again. But when his mother had called with the concern that Cassandra Carrigan might get lost if she tried to navigate the winding lakeshore roads, Michael knew he had to offer his help. He arranged to meet Cassie at a service station on Highway 19 so that she could follow him to Tessie's.

As he expected, his mother was waiting for them to arrive. She sat on the porch, wearing the blue dress she reserved for very special occasions. When she saw his Explorer pull into the driveway, she was up out of her chair and hustling down the steps. Instead of greeting him, she headed straight for Cassie's car, her cheeks flushed with enthusiasm.

The artist had barely climbed out of her minivan before Tessie was gushing. "You must be Cassandra. It is such an honor to meet you."

The smile Cassie gave his mother was warm and effervescent, very much like the ones she had given Michael when they'd been at the dinner together. When she smiled like that, his hormones made him want to forget he had a brain.

"I'm delighted to be here," he heard her say to Tessie.

"I am such a big fan of yours," his mother continued. "'Everlasting Love' is a wonderful tribute to marriage. When Michael told me he'd hired you to do my portrait—" she paused, choked with emotion "—I could hardly believe it! It is so very kind of you to take the time to come out here."

Michael felt like saying, "She's getting paid a hefty sum to come here," but held his tongue. He couldn't spoil Tessie's pleasure and it was obvious from the way her cheeks glowed and her eyes twinkled that this was a very special moment for her.

"I'm looking forward to working with you, Tessie." Cassandra responded to his mother's effusive praise with a graciousness that erased some of the bad feelings Michael harbored toward the artist. "I enjoy portrait work and to be able to do it in such lovely surroundings…" She looked around her, eyeing Tessie's lakeshore setting. "It's hardly going to seem like work at all. Any artist would love to have such a setting."

"It's where I've lived most of my life, so I guess it's fitting that it be the background for the portrait. At least that's what Michael thinks," Tessie said, finally giving him a casual glance.

"I agree," Cassie said, to his surprise.

"I was worried you might get lost on your way here. That's why I asked Michael to show you the way," Tessie continued.

Cassie looked then at Michael and all traces of warmth disappeared. It annoyed him that she had to place such a cool, guarded expression on her face every time she looked at him. What did she think? That he couldn't look at her without lusting after her?

With her usual ease, Tessie linked her arm in Cassie's and started toward the house. "Come inside. We'll get something cool to drink before we get started. It's such a glorious day it'd be a shame not to sit outside, don't you think?"

Cassie agreed. "Yes, and it's early enough in the season that the bugs haven't arrived."

They continued chatting as they walked toward the house, totally disregarding Michael, who still stood next to his Explorer. He might as well have been invisible.

"Hey. Does this mean I'm free to go?" His question had both of them turning.

"Go? Why would you leave?" Tessie asked, waving her arm in his direction, urging him to join them. "This portrait was your idea and I'm sure you're going to want to talk to Cassandra about it. Besides, I made you a pie."

Michael didn't want to stay and he could see that Cassie didn't want him to, either. It was there on her face—a face that he realized was as expressive as one of her portraits. It showed all of the emotions inside her pretty little head.

He wanted to tell his mother he was leaving, but she was giving him that "you'd better not be rude" look. And he supposed he should stay for at least a short visit to see what he was going to get for his money.

Only as it turned out, Cassie didn't even talk about her thoughts for Tessie's portrait. As the three of them sat outside on the patio facing the lake, she explained the procedure she would follow. Before beginning to sketch, it was important to her that she get to know her subject before trying to do justice to a portrait. So instead of discussing possible poses and taking photographs, which was what Michael thought she'd be doing, Cassie interviewed his mother.

When she pulled a microcassette recorder from her purse, Michael spoke up. "You plan to tape the conversation?"

"Yes. Tessie doesn't mind."

"Have you asked her?"

"Of course she's asked me, Michael," Tessie said in a slightly reprimanding tone. "We discussed it when we talked on the phone."

He eyed the small electronic device suspiciously. Cassie noticed.

"Do you have a problem with me recording our conversation?" she asked.

He shrugged. "It just doesn't seem necessary."

"I don't need to use it," she said, and started to put it back in her purse when Tessie stopped her.

"Don't be silly," she said, flapping her hand in midair. "Michael, you're not the one being interviewed. I am. Maybe you should go inside and get yourself a nice big piece of that strawberry pie."

"I thought you wanted me here."

"I'm sure Tessie and I will be just fine if you want to leave, Mr. McFerrin," Cassie added, the look on her face telling him she'd just as soon have him gone.

Michael resented the way she'd come into his mother's home and taken over. He wasn't going to leave, especially not if she was going to be asking Tessie questions that no doubt would include him.

"I'll stay," he told her, piercing her with a stare that warned her she wasn't going to push him around.

Tessie smiled and said to Cassie, "It's probably better if he does, because my memory isn't what it used to be."

"Don't worry about it, Tessie. The purpose of the interview is simply for us to get to know each other. Just think of it as two friends sharing thoughts."

So Michael sat silently, listening as Cassie inquired about his mother's personal life. Watching. And waiting. For Cassandra to overstep her bounds. He conceded that knowing a little more about Tessie would make it easier to do her portrait, but there was a limit as to what she needed to know.

It didn't take long for him to see that Cassandra was an excellent interviewer. And to his relief, she didn't ask anything that required an answer he wouldn't have wanted his mother to give. While the tape turned in the microcassette recorder, her pencil moved across the sketch pad she had on her lap.

From where he sat, he couldn't tell if she was taking notes or sketching his mother's face. He knew she did several pencil sketches before she did the pastel portrait.

He was relieved when she clicked the off button on the cassette recorder and flipped her sketch pad shut. "I think that's enough for today," she said.

"You need more lemonade." Tessie noted that Cassie's glass was empty.

"No, I'm fine. I really should be going."

"You don't have any time for pie?"

Michael thought she looked as if she wanted to leave, but to his surprise she said, "Maybe just a small piece."

Tessie's lips widened in delight. "Coffee, tea or more lemonade?"

"Lemonade is fine."

"All right. You sit here with Michael and I'll be right back."

As soon as she was gone, he said, "Thank you for taking the pie."

"I happen to like strawberries."

"So do I. We have something in common, but then we already knew that, didn't we?" he couldn't resist saying.

She shifted uncomfortably and turned her attention to the lake, where a sailboat drifted across the water. "We agreed to keep this professional, Mr. McFerrin."

"You can relax, Ms. Carrigan. I'm not going to jump your bones in my mother's home," he drawled, annoyed that he still found her attractive.

She didn't look at him, but continued to gaze out at the water. "This is a lovely spot. Did you grow up here?"

"Got my toes wet when I was four and have been in the water every summer since then."

"You were lucky. Not many kids have a private beach in their backyard," she stated with a hint of envy.

"That's not why I was lucky. Not many kids had a mother like Tessie," he told her.

Cassie looked at him and smiled. "She certainly enjoys life, doesn't she? I didn't expect that I'd be sketching an eighty-one-year-old who's more active than I am."

"I keep telling her she needs to slow down a bit, but she doesn't listen."

"She enjoys life."

"Yes, well I wish she'd enjoy it at a slower pace." He didn't tell her about the concerns he had for his mother's health. Although Tessie claimed she was fit as a fiddle, Michael knew she was at the time in her life when she needed to take things a bit more slowly.

"One of the things I'm going to want to capture in the portrait is her energy," Cassandra told him. "She has a zest for life you don't often find in young people, let alone an octogenarian."

"You ought to see her dance," he said with a grin.

"I'd like to. She said the Mums perform mostly around the holidays."

"You plan to be around six months from now?" he asked.

"I don't expect that it'll take me six months to do her portrait," she answered.

"Then you probably won't get to see the Mums dance."

She sighed. "I'm sorry to hear that because they sound like an amazing group of women."

"I'm sure Tessie will introduce you to them."

"How many of them are there?"

"Twelve. One of them lives next door." He glanced across the honeysuckle hedge that was in full bloom. "I'm surprised she's not here right now."

"You're surprised who isn't here?" Tessie asked over his shoulder. He jumped to his feet to help his mother with the serving tray she carried, taking it from her hands and setting it on the circular table.

"Nan. I was telling Ms. Carrigan that one of the Mums lives next door."

"Ms. Carrigan? Michael, I'm sure Cassandra doesn't expect you to be so formal, do you, dear?" Tessie asked as she refilled her glass with lemonade.

"Cassandra is fine," she answered.

Michael noticed that she didn't suggest he call her Cassie. No doubt she wanted no reminders of their dinner conversation.

While they ate strawberry pie in the shade of the floral umbrella perched over Tessie's table, some of the charm Michael had seen at the dating service dinner surfaced. And again he found his body responding to her nearness. Despite her assertion that she had no interest in him personally, he found he didn't want the afternoon to end.

When Cassie again commented on how lovely the Lake Minnetonka area was, Tessie took it as an opening to find out more about her guest. "Then you're not from this area?"

"No. I grew up in South Dakota."

"And where was that, dear?" Tessie asked.

"Mitchell."

"Where the corn palace is?" When Cassie nodded, Tessie went on. "It's been years since I was there. I know there used to be this wonderful doll museum in the center of town.''

"It's still there.''

"Oh, I just love dolls, as you may have noticed when we were inside the house. Do your folks still live in Mitchell?''

"No, they don't,'' she answered.

Michael could see by the way her eyes moved down to her plate and her fingers tightened around the fork that she wasn't going to elaborate. He knew that his mother had sensed her reluctance, as well, and was grateful she didn't probe any further.

"And did you always want to be an artist when you were growing up in South Dakota?'' Tessie asked.

Cassie's features softened as she looked up, a hint of a smile on her face. "Actually, when I was a child I wanted to be a veterinarian.''

That surprised Michael and it caused Tessie's eyes to light. "Well, isn't that a coincidence! You know Michael is a vet, don't you?''

"Oh yes, he's told me,'' she answered, her eyes meeting Michael's with a question. He guessed she was wondering if he'd told his mother where they had initially met.

He didn't say a word, but sat staring at her delicate frame, trying to picture her working at the clinic. The vision of her in his office in a lab coat was a pleasant one, but he could only imagine the difficulty she'd have trying to restrain a hundred and five pound Rottweiler.

"So you love animals,'' Tessie remarked, her eyes still twinkling.

"Doesn't everyone?'' she asked with a grin.

"Unfortunately, no," Michael answered soberly.

She gave him a look that said her remark wasn't to have been taken literally. Tessie didn't seem to notice. She continued chatting away. "Then you must have pets. Dogs or cats?"

"The apartment building where I live doesn't allow dogs," she answered. "I have a cat. An Abyssinian."

This time Tessie's eyes positively danced. "That's what my Cleo is." Michael could see by the look on his mother's face that she was quite taken with Cassandra Carrigan. Her next words proved it.

"Oh, Cassandra, I am so glad Michael brought you to me. I know we are going to get along just fine." Then she turned to him and said, "You made a wise choice, Michael."

He could almost see the wheels turning in his mother's head. It was time for him to steer the conversation in a different direction, "What made you change your mind about becoming a veterinarian?"

"In junior high school I did an internship with the local vet. After a couple of surgeries I knew I wasn't going into any kind of medicine." This time she hid her smile, but Michael could see it in her eyes.

"A wise decision," Tessie told her. "Talent like yours shouldn't be ignored. Your portraits have touched the lives of so many people it would have been a shame if you hadn't followed your heart."

"Thank you. That's very kind of you to say that," Cassie said with a grateful smile.

"I'm not being kind, dear. I'm telling the truth. It's wonderful to be able to patch up animals the way Michael does, but I'd hate to see you end up like him."

He groaned silently. "And what's that supposed to mean?"

"Just that you have so little free time." To Cassie she said, "I thought that when he became a vet instead of a physician, he wouldn't have to work all those crazy hours, but the life of an animal doctor can be very demanding of one's time. It's no wonder he hasn't had time to find—"

Michael cut her off quickly. "I don't think Cassandra wants to hear about the disadvantages of being a vet," he interrupted, worried that she was going to say he had no time for women. What he didn't need was for his mother to give her view of his personal life.

He was grateful when Cassie glanced at her watch and said, "I really ought to get going. Should we set up an appointment for our next meeting?"

"Let me get my calendar," Tessie said, pushing away from the table, but Michael stopped her.

"You sit, Mom. I'll get it for you."

"It's on the counter next to the phone," she told him.

He was relieved to escape for a few minutes. He found the calendar right away, but didn't return to the patio immediately. He chose to stand close to the window where he could look outside at Cassie Carrigan.

No matter how much he wanted to dismiss her as just another pretty face, he was finding it very difficult to ignore the feelings she aroused in him. He loved the sound of her laughter. When she chose to be, she could be vivacious and charming. It was a good thing he'd have no reason to see her once today was over.

The thought should have given him peace of mind.

It didn't.

Because as much as he hated to admit it, no matter how disinterested Cassie was in him, he only became more fascinated with her.

"A CLIENT GAVE ME two tickets for the new exhibit at the Walker. You interested in going with me on Sunday?" Claudia asked Cassie when they met for lunch at a small outdoor café near the river.

"Of course I'm interested, but I can't go on Sunday afternoon."

"What's more important than art?"

"I'm going to a tea at the arboretum with the Mums."

"The Mums?"

"They are these wonderful group of senior ladies who belong to a garden club on Lake Minnetonka. Not only do they grow flowers, they dance," Cassie answered in between bites of linguini.

"What do you mean they dance?"

"They tap-dance together in a chorus line. They even put on shows. Can you believe it? I mean, how wonderful for women that age to want to follow their hearts' desires."

"And where would you have met tap-dancing senior citizens?"

"That commissioned portrait work I just landed? She's one of them. Claudia, you wouldn't believe these women. There are twelve of them. All incredibly energetic and all wonderful tap dancers."

Claudia paused with her fork in midair. "And so the reason you're going to the arboretum with them is…"

"To spend some time with Tessie."

"Tessie being the eighty-one-year-old woman you're sketching?"

She nodded as she swallowed a bite of French bread. "I've been hanging out with her as much as possible this past week, because I want to get to know her so that I can do justice to her portrait. This isn't like the portraits I've done in the past. This one I'm being paid a lot of money to do and I want to make sure that I do the best job I can."

"So you think by going to a tea with twelve little old ladies you'll be inspired to great things?"

"It's all part of the process," Cassie told her, pushing aside the remainder of her linguini. "Besides, I like Tessie. She's an incredible woman. She has so many interesting stories to tell. Not to mention the great physical shape she's in. We went swimming and, would you believe, she can do more laps than I can?"

"Maybe you should send her to me. I've got this eighty-five-year-old guy that's a real dynamo," she quipped.

Cassie hadn't told Claudia that Tessie was the mother of one of Dinner Date's clients. Now she wished that, when she'd told her best friend about the commissioned portrait...she'd told Claudia it was Michael McFerrin who'd contacted her.

"Claudia, there's something I've been meaning to tell you," she began, not quite sure how to bring up the subject. "I know I let you think that this commission was a result of the exhibit at the senior citizen center."

"It wasn't?"

"It was, but..."

"But what? Has this Tessie been one of my clients

in the past?'' Her brow furrowed. ''I've had very few eighty-year-old women, Cassie. I think I would have remembered if...'' A frown furrowed her brow.

''It wasn't Tessie who was the client. It was her son. Michael McFerrin.''

Claudia nearly choked on her sandwich. ''He's the guy who called me three times trying to get your number.''

''I know.''

''You told me you didn't want anything to do with him.''

''I know, but I couldn't afford to turn down the money. You know what I'm getting for this work.''

Claudia took a sip of water, then said, ''You're right. You couldn't turn it down. But what a coincidence. Who would have thought you'd run into a client by displaying your work in a senior citizen center.'' She shook her head in amazement. ''Are you sure this is a good idea—I mean, he was rather aggressive in his pursuit of you.''

She shrugged. ''I've talked to Michael about it and he understands this is a professional association. Nothing more.''

''If I remember correctly, he is quite the man,'' Claudia said, rolling her eyes. ''Tall, nice body, great smile.''

Cassie didn't need any reminders of Michael McFerrin's looks. He'd been in her thoughts often enough thanks to Tessie. Every time the older woman mentioned her son, a vivid picture of a man with a dimpled grin that could make her heart skip a beat came to mind.

''You didn't tell him you work for me, did you?'' Claudia asked, tiny lines creasing her eyes.

"Of course not."

"Good, because I really don't want any of my clients to know I pay someone to keep the ball rolling. You know what I mean?"

She did. And it wasn't as if Cassie didn't benefit from the arrangement. She was able to enjoy an evening out without having the pressures of dating anyone.

"Don't worry. I'd never say anything," she assured her best friend. "No, Michael McFerrin thinks I was at the dinner for the same reason he was."

"About Michael. He wasn't..." Claudia began, then suddenly changed the subject. "Oh my gosh, I almost forgot to tell you. Donna Killigan wanted me to remind you that she's having a thirtieth birthday party for Terrance at the end of the month."

"All right, you've reminded me. Now what were you going to say about Michael McFerrin? He wasn't what?"

She looked around warily, as if wishing she hadn't opened her mouth. "He wasn't a typical client."

"What do you mean?"

She sighed and pushed her food around on her plate. "I can't say any more than that. You know anything a client tells me is confidential."

"But I'm an employee," Cassie insisted.

"No, you're a conversation starter. If you worked in the office, it'd be different, but we both agreed when we started our little arrangement that you'd keep your nose out of the business end."

Cassie knew she was right. Dinner Date clients paid good money to protect their privacy and it wouldn't be right for Claudia to reveal information about Michael without his permission. And the last thing Cassie wanted was for Claudia to suspect that she was even slightly interested in him.

Because she wasn't. So how come she couldn't stop thinking about him and wondering what it was Claudia knew that she didn't?

MICHAEL KNEW IT WAS INEVITABLE. He was an eligible bachelor, Cassie was a beautiful single woman. It was natural that Tessie would try to play matchmaker.

There was only one thing for Michael to do. Nip it in the bud before it went any further. That's why he made a special trip out to the lake to see his mother one evening—an evening when he knew she would be alone.

"Michael, come in. What a nice surprise," she said, greeting him with her usual hug and kiss on the cheek. "Why didn't you call and let me know you were coming? I would have made something special for dinner."

"And asked Cassandra to stay?"

"I could have if I had known you were going to be coming over," she admitted with that matchmaking motherly grin of hers. "She's such a dear, Michael. We've been having so much fun getting to know each other."

"I'm glad to hear that. When is she going to start the portrait?"

"Oh, she has. Not on paper." She tapped her forehead. "Up here. She's letting all of her thoughts and impressions take shape. It takes time, Michael. You can't hurry art."

"It's obvious she can't," he noted.

Tessie clicked her tongue. "Michael, I hope that wasn't intended the way it sounded."

He sighed. "I'm sure she'll do a wonderful job with the portrait, Mom. I wouldn't have hired her if I didn't think she would. But I think we should talk about Cassandra Carrigan."

"Fine. Sit down and I'll get us something cool to drink," she said, opening the refrigerator. "Did you know she's a widow?"

"Emmet Sandberg mentioned it to me."

She pulled a pitcher of iced tea out and set it on the table. "Apparently her husband died before they could even celebrate their first anniversary. Such a sad thing to happen to any young bride, but to someone like Cassie..." she sighed. "Well, it just breaks my heart to think about it. She's such a sweet thing. She deserves to be happy."

"Happy as in married happy?" he asked with a wry grin.

She poked him playfully. "I didn't say married, I said *happy.*" She pulled two tall glasses from the cupboard and set them on the table.

"Well, before you go getting your hopes up that I might be the one who could fill her life with blissful harmony, there's something I think you need to know," he said as he watched his mother fill the glasses with tea.

"And what's that?"

"Cassandra Carrigan and I aren't singing from the same songbook."

"Oh, Michael," she pooh-poohed him with a flap of her hand. "And how would you know? You've only seen the woman twice."

"That's where you're wrong," he admitted.

Puzzlement wrinkled her trusting features. "I don't understand."

He took a sip of the iced tea. "Remember that dating service dinner you set me up with a few weeks back? It just so happens that Cassandra Carrigan was one of the guests at the dinner."

That produced a gasp from his mother. "No!"

"Yes."

"Why didn't she tell me?"

"Maybe because she's embarrassed to admit it," he suggested. "We spent a good portion of the evening talking to each other and I thought things were going pretty well between us, so I decided to call Dinner Date the following Monday and ask for them to arrange another meeting, this time with just the two of us."

"And she didn't want to meet you again?"

"Bingo. She wasn't interested."

"That can't be!" Tessie stated emphatically.

"I appreciate your faith in my ability to attract beautiful women, but I'm afraid it's true. If I had any doubt that it was, Cassandra soon erased it when we met to discuss your portrait. She told me our relationship was strictly professional."

She sank down onto a kitchen chair, disappointment clouding her eyes. "But..." She was unable to finish her sentence.

"It's all right, Mom. I know you like Cassandra and you think that we'd be a good match, but you see, it's just not meant to be."

She sat silent, looking a bit forlorn, and Michael felt anger toward Cassandra Carrigan bubble up inside him.

Then Tessie said, "I don't think you should take it

personally. It could be that she has never gotten over her first husband."

He shrugged. "You might be right."

"Of course I'm right. Otherwise she'd be a crazy fool not to want to go out with someone like you. And she's not crazy. Heartbroken, maybe, but crazy, no."

Michael wasn't sure he liked his mother's explanation any better than he'd liked Cassie's rejection, although it made sense. He discovered, however, that the thought of Cassie pining away over a love that was gone disturbed him.

As he drove away from his mother's, he tried not to think about Cassie at all, but it didn't make sense. Why would she go to a dating service looking for love if she was still hung up on her late husband?

He thought his visit with his mother would clear the air in more ways than one. Now he'd discovered that instead of forgetting about Cassie the artist, he was determined to learn more about her.

Chapter Six

"It has been agreed and voted upon that the thirteenth annual Mum holiday show will be the first weekend in December." Louella pounded her gavel on Mildred Bennett's dining room table. "Next item up for discussion is the courtship of Dr. Mac. Dorothy, I believe you have something to tell us."

"I do." She beamed proudly as she stood. "A lot has happened since we last met. Thanks to Violet leaving her scarf in Dr. Mac's car, we didn't have to follow plan B. Michael and Cassandra have met."

Delightful sounds resonated around the table.

"Tessie probably can tell us more," she said, then sat down, yielding the floor to her fellow Mum.

Tessie stood. "It's true. They have met and at first I thought it looked good. But I'm afraid there's a snag." That was met by a collective sigh. "This might be more of a challenge than we expected."

"The boat ride didn't work?" Agnes inquired.

"I did just as Francine suggested. I had Cassie come over when Michael was working on the speedboat. There she was with her long legs and bare shoulders and all he could do was look at that dirty old motor."

"He didn't appreciate a young woman in shorts?" Edith's wrinkled jaw fell open.

Tessie clicked her tongue. "She could have had two heads and he wouldn't have noticed. And when I suggested he take her for a ride and show her the lake, he told me he couldn't because he didn't have the right spark plugs."

Several comments could be heard, including, "What's wrong with the man? You don't suppose he's…"

To which Tessie responded vehemently, "No! He's not!"

"If she came over in short shorts and a tiny little top, you'd think he'd be falling all over himself to impress her," another remarked, which prompted several murmurs of speculation.

Tessie lifted her hands to quiet the room. "There's a good reason he's not noticing. She's already told him she's not interested."

"When?" Francine demanded.

"Remember Dinner Date?" A collective nod had her continuing. "Cassandra Carrigan was one of the participants."

That elicited several gasps. "So they've met before?"

"At the dinner."

"Then she must have seen how well mannered he is," Louella pointed out.

"And how charming," another said.

"Of course she did," Tessie agreed. "And Michael was very interested in her. Only when he called to set up another meeting, she told the dating service director she wasn't interested in him."

"I can't believe it!"

"Me, neither."

"Maybe she wasn't feeling well that night."

"Did she have her glasses on?

"Does she wear glasses?"

"Ladies!" Louella pounded the gavel. "Let Tessie speak."

"I have a theory. It may or not be true, but I'm wondering if maybe the reason she's not interested in Michael is because she's still carrying a torch for her husband. She was widowed at a very young age, you know."

"That has to be it. Why else would any woman not fall for Dr. Mac?" Mildred asked the rhetorical question.

"Her heart's still broken," Nan said somberly.

"Then we're just going to have to figure out a way to help her mend it," Louella remarked.

"It's not going to be easy," Tessie warned.

"That's what they said about us when we wanted to start the dance line." Louella smiled smugly. "Anyone think we can't do it?"

Not a single woman raised her hand.

"She just needs to see what a nice boy he is," Agnes pointed out.

"That's true. You should tell her about all the nice things he does for you," Francine suggested.

"Better yet. Have her see them," Betty Jean interjected.

"What she needs is to see him doing something nice for his mother that also shows off all those manly muscles," Edith said with a wink. "Why not have her over when he's cutting the grass? He usually takes off his shirt when he's pushing that mower around, doesn't he?"

"Oh yes, he does." Tessie's eyes sparkled with maternal pride. "But he doesn't usually cut my lawn. He hired Robbie Watson to do it for me every Monday this summer."

"Then you'll just have to figure out a reason why Robbie can't do it on Monday. Maybe he's going away on vacation," Edith said with an innocent look in her eye.

Francine shook her head. "School's still in session."

"Could be he's sick," Betty Jean added.

"Oh, I couldn't lie," Tessie said.

"Tessie, this is about Michael's happiness," Louella reminded her. "And it's not a big lie. Just a little white one. And you wouldn't really have to say why he can't do it. Just tell Michael Robbie's not available this week."

Tessie didn't speak, but sat thinking. Finally she said, "I do remember Robbie's mother saying that with final exams coming up he might have to postpone cutting the grass."

"There you go. Final exams." Agnes rubbed her hands together. "Problem solved. It'll be perfect. A good-looking young man mowing his mother's grass without his shirt on." She gave a tender little sigh. "Even a brokenhearted widow isn't immune to beefcake."

"I'D LIKE TO BEGIN SKETCHING," Cassie told Tessie as they sat sipping iced tea in the shade of her backyard.

"But I so enjoy just sitting around chatting. Summer is so short in Minnesota. It seems a shame to spend it working indoors,'' Tessie said as they sat on a small bench in the middle of her rose garden.

''I could sketch you out here,'' Cassie suggested.

''With my roses?''

''I've been thinking about having you sit in the gazebo.'' She glanced at the wooden structure painted white. Potted red geraniums dangled between the intricately carved columns, making it the perfect foil for Tessie's energetic personality.

''Oh, Michael would like that. It was a birthday gift from him,'' Tessie told her, the usual sparkle lighting her face whenever her son's name was mentioned.

And it had been mentioned often. She supposed it was natural. He was Tessie's only son and it was obvious that she was very proud of him.

Cassie had learned as much about Michael McFerrin as she'd learned about Tessie. And it was beginning to be a bit too much, because instead of growing bored with the subject, she found herself becoming more curious about the veterinarian and thinking about him far too often. She was here because of Tessie, not Michael.

That's why she was relieved to arrive at the lake today and find Tessie alone. On her previous visit he'd been down by the water, working on the engine of the inboard motorboat. Tessie had told her it was his boat. Just as it was his pair of water skis in the canopied lift on the opposite side of the wooden dock. He loved the water. He also loved lemon meringue pie, pot roast with gravy and fresh walleye caught and cooked the very same day.

It was more information than Cassie needed. Nor did she need to have Tessie arranging for the two of them to spend time together. Like suggesting that Michael take Cassie for a boat ride. Fortunately, engine problems had put an end to that idea. Cassie had said a silent prayer of thanks for faulty spark plugs. She didn't want to be alone with Michael and, judging by the way he had greeted her, the feeling was mutual.

Which was why she thought it would be wiser to whisk this sweet little old lady away from the lake and back to her studio for the portrait work. Only wiser for her emotional state, not better for this particular pastel. The more she discovered about Tessie, the more convinced she was that to do the portrait right, it needed to be done here at the lake.

"When would you like to start?" Tessie asked, interrupting her thoughts.

Cassie pulled her planner from her purse. "How does Monday afternoon work for you?"

"That's my bridge afternoon," Tessie answered.

"Okay, how about Tuesday morning?"

"The Mums are going to begin practicing for their Christmas show. Maybe you want to come watch?"

"They practice every Tuesday?"

"And Thursday."

Which eliminated those two mornings, Cassie acknowledged silently. "Then how about Wednesday morning?"

Tessie shook her head. "Swimming lessons."

"You're taking swimming lessons?"

"No, I give them."

It shouldn't have surprised Cassie. She had discovered that Tessie McFerrin was a remarkable woman in more ways than one.

Cassie looked up from her day planner. "Maybe

you should tell me what time is good for you and we'll take it from there.''

"I'd better get my calendar so I don't forget anything," she said, rising to her feet. "You just sit here and I'll be right back."

Cassie took the opportunity to once again survey the surroundings, thinking of possible locations that might be a backdrop for Tessie's portrait. As she glanced around the beautifully landscaped yard, she saw an old tire swing hanging from an oak. It would make a great setting for a sketch of a little boy swinging on an old tire suspended from a tree.

Again her thoughts turned to Michael. He'd probably swung from the tire on a lazy summer afternoon like this. She bet he'd been a cute little kid and could imagine him running and jumping off the end of the dock into the lake. She closed her eyes, willing herself to stop thinking about the man.

Yet she couldn't forget the way his tall, lean body had looked in a pair of cutoff denim shorts and a faded blue T-shirt. He'd said very little to her the last time she'd seen him, other than the usual courtesies extended to his mother's guests, but there had been that look in his eye, a rather furtive twinkle that indicated he and Cassie had a secret. She knew it was there because of Dinner Date, reminding her that for one night she'd found him very attractive—no matter how much she wanted to deny it.

"Here we are, dear," Tessie said, coming toward her. "It's a good thing I went inside. Michael had called and left a message."

Cassie wanted to ask what the message was but used every ounce of willpower she possessed to act disinterested.

Tessie sat down beside her, the calendar on her lap. "Oh, my. I didn't realize I had booked so many things," she said on a little giggle.

Cassie couldn't believe it, either. Every square had writing on it. Tessie had used several different colors of ink so that now her calendar looked like a kaleidoscope of scribbled codes.

"It looks as if the only time I have free is in the evenings. I hate to even have to ask if that will work for you." She gave Cassie an apologetic look.

Cassie was a morning person. Usually, if she didn't get an early start, it didn't get done. When she didn't answer right away, Tessie took it as an objection.

"I'm sorry. I shouldn't have asked. I'm sure you have friends you want to see in the evening. That's your free time. You don't want to be spending it with an old lady."

"No, it's all right. If evenings work best for you, we'll do evenings."

Tessie bestowed the most angelic of smiles on Cassie. "Why, aren't you the sweetest thing? Thank you, dear, for being so accommodating."

"It's not a problem. That's one of the perks of being an artist. I can usually arrange my schedule to my convenience. And to be perfectly honest, evenings work better for me, too. You see, I have another job."

"You do?"

"Yes. I do temporary work on an on-call basis."

"Surely you don't have to?" She covered her mouth as if scolding herself. "Forgive me for saying that. I didn't mean to pry into your financial status."

"It's all right. I think it's pretty well-known that most artists have day jobs until they get established in their field. I'm hoping that 'Everlasting Love' will open enough doors for me so that I can give up mine.''

"I hope that, too. I hate to think of you working two jobs. It must leave very little time for a social life."

"I do work a lot," she admitted.

"You and Michael." Tessie clicked her tongue. "I'll tell you the same thing I tell him. You're only young once, so enjoy it."

Cassie couldn't help but smile. She had a feeling that it didn't matter what age Tessie was, she would always enjoy life. "I think that's good advice and obviously you've always followed it."

"I have. I say grab all the gusto you can." She punched the air with her fist and smiled. "Only at my age the gusto doesn't include men. I figure it's time I let the young ones like you have a chance. You do manage to find time for romance, I hope?"

Cassie sighed. "I'm afraid my time for romance has come and gone."

"You mustn't say that, dear." Tessie placed a hand on her forearm. "I know you've suffered a great loss in your life."

Cassie suspected that Emmet Sandberg or one of the other seniors she'd sketched had probably told everyone at the center that she was a widow. "It was a long time ago," she said, hoping to have the subject end there. "And life goes on."

"Yes, it does," Tessie agreed. "But the pain of losing someone you love goes on, too. It may ease a bit with time, but it never really goes away."

Not for Cassie it didn't, but then her pain was not that of a typical widow. She hadn't just suffered a loss; she'd suffered a betrayal.

"I'm sorry, Tessie, but if you don't mind, I'd rather not talk about that time in my life," she told the older woman, reluctant to talk about love and marriage.

She'd deliberately allowed people to believe that the reason she hadn't started dating again was because she'd lost her true love. It was much easier to let people assume that she was brokenhearted rather than admit to the truth—that her husband of only two years had left not only a wife behind when he died, but a lover, a child and a pile of debts.

"I know how difficult it can be, but you mustn't let your husband's death stop you from living, Cassie," Tessie said gently.

Cassie simply said, "When he died, a piece of me died, too." What she didn't say was that the piece of her that had died was the part of her that said she could trust her heart to love.

"I know what you're feeling, dear. When my Frank died, I thought I couldn't go on. He was my first and last love. I didn't want any other after he was gone, so I lived my life dedicated to his memory, passing up chances that would never come my way again."

"And do you regret it?"

"I do, yes, because life is too short to spend it wishing for something you can't have. I'd hate to see that happen to you." For the first time Cassie saw a sadness in Tessie that threatened to chase away her cheerful spirit.

"I appreciate your concern, Tessie, but the truth is I'm happy being single," she told her.

"That's good. Every woman should be able to live alone, but it doesn't mean you *have* to live alone."

Cassie smiled. "You're right."

"So I want you to promise me that should an opportunity come your way, you won't miss it because you're trying to live in the past. I'm not saying you have to go looking for it. Just don't ignore it if it happens into your life.''

Cassie didn't expect love to happen, not when she was doing everything in her power to avoid it. ''I'll stay open to possibilities,'' she said to appease the older woman. ''Now what evening next week should I come over?''

''Well, let me see.'' She paused as she pondered over her calendar. Then she said, ''How about Monday?''

''Monday will be just fine.''

''WHAT HAPPENED TO YOU?''

It was not the kind of greeting Michael expected from his mother. ''Hi, Mom. Nothing's happened, why?''

''You look as if you haven't shaved in two days!''

''I haven't. I just got back from the boundary waters with Jack. I told you we were going up there this weekend, didn't I?''

''Yes, but...'' She tried to hide her disgust but failed.

''I guess I should have gone home first, but I was already out this way and I didn't see much point in driving all the way to town so I could turn around and come back out here.'' She was looking at him as if that's exactly what he should have done. ''You did say you wanted me to stop by on Monday, right?''

She nodded. ''To cut the grass, but I didn't think you'd be coming until after dinner.''

''Don't worry about it. You don't need to feed me. I'll cut the grass and take my mangy body home and everything will be fine," he said with a grin and a wink. "Is the garage unlocked?"

"The garage? Oh, you need to get the mower. Yes, it's open," she told him, eyes roving over him critically. "Is that blood on your shirt?"

He glanced down. "Probably. We cleaned quite a few fish." Seeing the look of distaste on her face, he said, "I might have a clean shirt in the truck. You want me to check my bag?"

She grimaced. "I guess it doesn't matter. You'll probably just take it off anyway."

"Take it off?"

"While you cut the grass. It's hot."

"Not that hot."

"It will be once you start pushing that mower around."

"It's self-propelled. I don't think you have to worry about me suffering from heat exhaustion."

Her eyes made another critical study of him before she said, "Maybe you want to take a shower and put on some clean clothes."

"To cut the grass?" He didn't get it. Not since he'd been a teenager had she fussed over how he looked.

"I was just thinking that Otto and Nan might be out on their deck having dinner." She glanced nervously toward the neighbor's yard.

"You think they care if I have on grubby clothes?"

"I'm just trying to be considerate. It is the dinner hour, after all," she answered.

"Relax. I'm sure Otto's and Nan's appetites won't be ruined because I'm wearing the same clothes to cut the grass that I wore in the boundary waters."

"I suppose you're right," she said, but he could see she wasn't happy with the way he looked.

Several times as he cut the grass he looked back at the house and saw her watching him, a look of worry on her face. It wasn't until he'd almost finished the front yard that he discovered the true reason for her concern.

As he trimmed the edges of the sidewalk, he saw a minivan pull into the driveway. Sitting behind the wheel was Cassandra Carrigan.

Michael felt the familiar rush of adrenaline he was coming to expect whenever he saw the artist. She played havoc with his hormones. He recognized it as a purely physical thing. If she had simply accepted his request to have dinner with him, they could have shared a few good times, he would have gotten her out of his system and then he could have forgotten about her.

But she hadn't wanted to see him again. He guessed that was probably what was behind this surge of excitement he felt whenever he was around her. He'd had very little experience with rejection and it seemed to only increase his interest in her.

Not that he wanted her to know he was intrigued. As she parked her minivan next to his Explorer, he turned his attention back to the lawn, acting as if her presence was of no concern to him.

But it was hard to ignore someone as lovely as Cassandra Carrigan. No matter how hard he tried to keep from glancing in her direction, he couldn't help himself. He watched her climb out of her car, a large sketch pad under her arm. He saw her walk with Tessie past the flower gardens, pausing to admire the early summer blooms.

Then he saw her climb the steps to the gazebo where she fussed over his mother as she decided what pose would be best for the portrait. Back and forth across the grass Michael went with the mower, and each time he passed the gazebo he glanced at the pair of them.

Or more correctly he glanced at the artist inside the shelter. Her long blond hair was tied back with a scarf, her face expressionless as her eyes darted back and forth between Tessie and the sketch pad. So engrossed was she in her work that not even when he mowed the grass around the gazebo, did her attention waver from her subject.

Michael thought he might be able to leave without ever saying a word to her, but as he was dumping the mulched clippings on Tessie's compost heap, his mother called out to him.

"Michael, you must come say hello to Cassandra."

Reluctantly he made his way over to the gazebo where Cassie sat like a princess, waiting for her subjects to come pay homage. She smiled politely, but he could see from the way she glanced down that pretty little nose of hers that she didn't want to have to make small talk with him. Which only annoyed him and had him climbing the steps, mangy clothes and all.

"Whew, I am tired this evening," Tessie said after the three of them had exchanged niceties about the weather. "If you don't mind, Michael, I think I'll go inside and let you show Cassandra to her car."

His mother couldn't have been more obvious. First she'd tried to get him to shower and change into clean clothes, now she was going to go inside and leave him to say good-night to Cassie. He wondered if Robbie was really studying for final exams or if this was all a part of her plan to throw him and Cassie to-gether.

He suspected the artist knew what she was up to, also, for she said, "It's all right, Tessie. I can find my own way out."

"No, no. Michael will take care of you, won't you, dear?" She gave him a woeful look, then again said she was tired and ambled toward the house.

When she was gone, he said, "She's not very sub-tle, is she?"

"I don't know what you mean," Cassandra an-swered.

He smiled wryly. "Come on. We both know she's been trying to get us together."

"Has she?" She gathered up her sketch pad and hoisted it under her arm. "I hadn't noticed. Good night, Mr. McFerrin." She left the gazebo and started across the yard.

"She's not tired. She stays up later than both of us," he called after her.

She paused then and turned around to say, "That may be true, but I thought she looked a bit pale. You should check on her before you leave." Then she turned and began walking again.

Irritation stung his nerves. Now she was telling him how to take care of his mother. "Good night, Ms. Carrigan," he called out to her, but she didn't turn around, just kept on walking.

Michael put away the lawn mower and went inside the house. "Mom?"

"In the living room, dear," she responded feebly.

He found her sitting on the sofa with her feet up, talking on the phone. She placed her hand over the receiver and said, "It's Louella."

"I thought you were going to bed," he said quietly, noticing that she was still dressed.

"I am, but I have to talk to Louella about Mum business," she told him.

"Well, I'm going to leave. I put the mower in the garage."

She nodded, blew him a kiss and went back to her conversation.

As Michael passed the mirror in the hallway, he saw just how grubby he must have looked to Cassandra. No wonder she hadn't wanted to talk to him. As he drove home, there was one thought that kept returning to his mind. He should have listened to his mother and cleaned up.

THE FOLLOWING MORNING Michael was in the middle of examining a Great Dane when Jenny interrupted.

"Dr. Mac, your mother's on line one and she sounds upset."

"Thank you, I'll be right there," he told her, then excused himself from the Great Dane's owner and went to his office.

"Mom? What's wrong?"

"I'm not feeling well, Michael. Something's not right."

"What's not right, Mom?"

"I don't know. I'm tired. I'm going to go back to bed. I shouldn't have bothered you."

Before he could tell her it was no bother, she'd hung up. He hurried out to the front desk and said to Jenny, "Can Lynn take my appointments for the rest of the morning?" As soon as Jenny had checked the schedule and assured him it wasn't a problem, he told her, "I'm going to go check on Tessie, but before I do, would you get me Otto Holmgren's number?"

By the time Michael had finished with the Great Dane, Jenny had looked up the phone number of Tessie's next-door neighbor. Before leaving the clinic, Michael called him.

"Otto, it's Dr. Mac. I just had a call from my mom. She said she's not feeling well. I'm on my way over there, but would you go check on her for me?"

"Oh, Dr. Mac. I'm glad you called. The ambulance is there now."

"The ambulance?" Michael's heart beat so loudly in his chest he thought the whole office must be hearing it.

"Yes, that artist friend of Tessie's called 9-1-1."

"Why? What's wrong?"

"I don't know, but I think they're taking your mother to the hospital."

"Which one?"

"I'm not sure, but if you hold on, I'll have the wife run over and find out for you."

It only took a few minutes for Michael to get the answer to his question, but it was the longest few minutes of his life.

"They're taking her to Methodist. They think it's her heart," Otto said, his own voice wobbly at the thought.

"Thanks, Otto. I'm on my way. Will you run over and tell my mother I'll meet her there?" he said, then hung up the phone.

Chapter Seven

Cassie was waiting just inside the hospital entrance when Michael arrived. Gone was the charming, devil-may-care smile that usually graced his handsome face. In its place was a frightened, haggard look of concern.

''Where is she?'' he asked as she walked toward him.

''She's going to be all right. She was in the emergency room, but they wanted her in the CICU just as a precaution.''

''Cardiac intensive care? Then it is her heart?''

''They didn't say. I did talk to one of the nurses, though, and she said all of your mother's vital signs are good,'' Cassie told him as she led him toward the elevators.

''No thanks to me.'' He raked a hand over his closely cropped hair.

''What's that supposed to mean?''

''You were there last night. She told me she didn't feel well and what did I do? Nothing.'' He shook his head in remorse. ''I thought she was playing match-maker—you know, saying she was tired and going to bed so that we would be left alone.''

"I thought the same thing," Cassie admitted, although it was obvious her admission gave him no comfort.

"She's eighty-one. I should have known that when she said she was tired, something was wrong. She's never tired. You've seen the way she gets around. She dances in a chorus line, for Pete's sake."

This time Cassie didn't try to comfort him with a response. They stepped into an elevator and she waited for the doors to slide shut before speaking again.

"She's going to be all right," she tried to reassure him, but she could see her words were of little comfort to him so she remained silent the rest of the way.

At the nursing station, Michael found out as much information as was available and was told the doctor would be out shortly to talk to him. It was suggested that Michael take a seat in the lounge at the end of the hall, but he chose to stand outside his mother's door.

Cassie waited with him until the doctor came out. "I'm Michael McFerrin, Tessie's son. Is she going to be all right?"

"She's resting comfortably," the doctor answered, after introducing himself and shaking Michael's hand. "Do you know how long she's been having the pains in her chest?"

"I didn't know she was having pains in her chest," he answered.

"She says she's had a cold and right now we've found nothing to think it's anything else. We'll keep her overnight to be sure," he told Michael.

"If it's just a cold, why is she in the cardiac unit?"

Michael asked the same question that was on Cassie's mind.

"The paramedics detected an irregularity in her heartbeat on the way in here."

"What caused that?"

"That's what we need to find out. The good news is that so far, we haven't found anything to give us concern. Her heart and lungs sound normal, but we'll run a few more tests this afternoon."

"As a precaution?"

The doctor was guarded with his response. "She is eighty-one. She appears to be in excellent health, but we want to make sure we haven't missed anything."

"I appreciate that. When can I see her?"

"You can go in now."

Not wanting to intrude on their private moment, Cassie told Michael she'd wait in the lounge while he visited with Tessie. As she sat thumbing through a women's magazine, she found it difficult to concentrate on any of the articles.

She kept seeing the look that had been on Michael's face when he had arrived at the hospital. Had it been anyone but him in such obvious distress, she would have put her arms around him in a comforting gesture.

But she didn't feel as if she could do that with him, not after everything that had happened. She wished now that their relationship had started off on a different foot. She should have never flirted with him at the Dinner Date event. When he'd responded to that flirting, she'd rejected him. Then there was the business about him tricking her into meeting him at the senior citizen center. Was it any wonder that every time they were together there was an awkwardness between them? Not even gentle, sweet Tessie could change that.

"She's asking for you."

Michael's voice broke into her thoughts, startling her to her feet. "Should I go in?"

"You'll have to wait until the nurses are finished with her. She suggested I buy you lunch while we wait...that is, if you want to wait."

"I do." Although she wasn't sure having lunch with Michael was a good idea. Being with the man did funny things to her equilibrium. She thought if she was smart, she'd tell him she'd come back later this afternoon to see Tessie.

However, today she wasn't feeling so smart. Her emotions had a pretty good grip on her common sense, and they were telling her to spend more time with this man who only a short while ago had revealed a vulnerable side she'd never expected to see. So she said, "Lunch would be nice."

He smiled then, the kind of smile she hadn't seen since that the night at the art exhibit when he'd made it perfectly clear that he'd hoped they could pick up where they'd left off at the dinner party. After she'd told him in no uncertain terms that it was business and business only between them, that smile had disappeared.

Now it was back and she felt her body responding to it. She reminded herself that nothing had changed. He was still a customer paying for a portrait.

Yet as they sat at one of the small tables in the hospital cafeteria, it didn't feel like a customer-client relationship. Despite being in a large lunchroom with hundreds of medical professionals surrounding them, it felt as if they were the only two people in the room.

They talked as easily as they had the night of the Dinner Date party, making Cassie feel as if they were old friends.

Only they weren't friends at all. Other than one evening of flirting with each other, they'd hardly talked. Yet there was almost an intimacy in their conversation. Cassie found it very easy to talk to Michael. She decided it had to be because he was a good listener, although by the time they left the lunchroom, she realized that he'd told her just as much about himself.

"Thank you for lunch. It wasn't bad for hospital food, was it?" she said as they left the cafeteria and headed back to the CICU.

"No, it was surprisingly good. But you don't need to thank me. It's the least I could do considering what you did for my mother. She told me you were the one who called the ambulance."

"I'm glad I was there to help out."

"So am I. She said you weren't scheduled to go over to the house until this evening."

"I wasn't, but I wanted to take some photographs of the gazebo in the morning light."

"You didn't get your pictures, I take it?"

She shook her head. "They can wait."

As they passed a bank of phones, he paused. "I need to call the clinic. You go ahead and I'll meet you upstairs."

"Sure, no problem," she said, then crossed the lobby to the row of elevators. While she waited, she couldn't keep her eyes from drifting back toward the phones. Only Michael wasn't there.

She glanced at the gift shop across the hall. There she saw his dark head through the glass window and watched it as he moved toward the refrigerated flower case. A chime alerted her to the fact that an elevator was ready for boarding. Just before she stepped inside the open doors, she saw Michael lift a huge bouquet of roses from the case.

That's why it was no surprise when, a few minutes after she'd arrived at Tessie's bedside, Michael came in carrying a vase with a dozen yellow roses.

"Oh, Michael, they're lovely," the bedridden Tessie declared in a weak voice.

"They're as close as I can take you to being at home smelling the roses from your own garden," he said as she set the flowers on the ledge near the window.

"Aren't they beautiful, Cassie?" Tessie continued to gush over the flowers.

"Yes, they are." She walked over to sniff the bouquet.

"They really brighten the room, don't you think?" Tessie added.

"Yes. Flowers will do that. They can make a not-so-nice day turn into something very special," she agreed with another appreciative glance at the roses.

Cassie wished she had gone home and returned later in the day, for it was obvious that Tessie needed Michael's presence, not hers. As Cassie watched the affectionate banter between mother and son, she felt a bit envious. She hadn't had that kind of a relationship with her own parents. To see so much respect between Michael and Tessie made her realize just what she'd missed.

After only a few minutes, she made a graceful exit. Later that day as she worked on her sketch of Tessie, it wasn't the octogenarian who occupied her thoughts, but her son. What an interesting man he was. Too interesting, she thought, and decided it would be best if she remembered why she was seeing him at all.

"ALL RIGHT, LADIES, this meeting will now come to order," Louella said with a clap of her gavel on Tessie's nightstand. All eleven of the Mums were gathered around Tessie as she rested in her bedroom. The window was open with a gentle summer breeze off the lake wafting the lace curtain.

"We should be downstairs at the dining room table," Tessie told them. "I feel fine."

"We know you do, but you know what Dr. Mac said," Louella reminded her.

Tessie expelled a puff of air in a sound of disgust and flapped her hand. "He's an animal doctor, not a cardiologist."

Agnes smoothed her covers. "There, there now. It's only for a couple of days. Next week you'll be back at the center with us, tapping away."

"Yes, but in the meantime we have work to do," Tessie informed them.

"You said we needed to act swiftly, and that's why I called the meeting," Louella said.

"Yes. We need to strike while the iron's hot," Tessie told them.

"Are things heating up with Dr. Mac and Cassie?" Edith asked with wide eyes.

"As much as I hate being sick, I have to admit that me having to make a trip to the hospital did warm things up a bit," Tessie reported with a twinkle in her eye.

"Ooh, do tell us," several voices urged.

Tessie relayed the details with great pleasure, not

leaving out a single look shared by her son and the artist.

"Oh, we are making progress, aren't we." Francine rubbed her hands together in delight.

"Yes. Now here's what I think we should do next," Tessie said with a sly twinkle in her eye.

SINCE THE DOCTORS HAD ADVISED Tessie to take it easy and get some rest once she was back home, Cassie postponed the sittings they had scheduled and accepted a temporary assignment answering phones at a customer service center.

By Friday evening she was happy to have the weekend to herself. Except for a Dinner Date assignment on Saturday, she planned to do nothing except work in her studio.

That's where she was on Saturday morning when the doorbell rang. A glance out her second-story window revealed a florist's delivery truck was out front. Thinking it had to be for one of her neighbors who wasn't home, she pressed the intercom. "Yes?"

"Delivery for a Cassandra Carrigan."

"Second floor, first door on your right," she answered, then pressed the button to unlock the lobby door.

She was waiting for the man when he arrived with a long, rectangular box. "Thanks," she said, handing him a tip before closing the door.

She carried the box over to her kitchen table where she untied the silver cord and lifted the lid. Inside were the most beautiful roses she'd ever seen. They were a luscious shade of coral and every one was perfectly formed. She lifted the small white envelope and pulled out the card.

It read, "For Cassandra, just in case you're having a 'not so nice' day." It was signed, "Dr. Mac."

She sighed dreamily as she sank down onto a chair and gazed at the flowers, inhaling their heady scent. It had been a long time since any man had sent her roses. Was it any wonder she felt a little breathless?

Which was exactly what seeing Dr. Mac's name had done to her. It had taken her breath away. And made her a little weak-kneed. And tickled the little spot inside her that she'd thought no longer existed. She didn't want to feel any of those things.

However, until she knew the reason for his sending the flowers, it was silly to read anything into the gesture. He could have simply sent them because he was grateful for help in getting Tessie to the hospital. Or he could have sent them because, no matter what they'd agreed upon when she'd accepted the commission, he still regarded her as a single woman who'd attended a dinner for singles looking to meet other singles.

She hoped it was the first reason and not the latter. She didn't need the added complication of Tessie's son pursuing her on a personal level. As she put the flowers in water, she realized that there was only one thing to do. Until she made it perfectly clear that she was not a single woman looking to find love, she couldn't expect Dr. Mac to give up his pursuit.

She picked up the phone and called Claudia. "We need to talk."

"DOESN'T SHE LOOK WONDERFUL?"

For once Cassie wasn't unhappy that Michael was at his mother's house when she arrived for the sitting. The sooner they cleared the air about the flowers and his misconception that she was a client of Dinner Date, the sooner she could get back to the task at hand, Tessie's portrait.

"You look like you're feeling much better than the last time I saw you," Cassie told the older woman, aware of Michael's eyes on her as she sat down on one of the patio chairs.

"There's nothing wrong with me, is there, Michael?"

"The doctors say she can start tapping those toes again whenever she wants," he confirmed.

Cassie reached for Tessie's hand and gave it a squeeze. "I'm glad to hear that. I'm looking forward to seeing you dance."

"You will. And soon." She chuckled. "I've choreographed a very special number for the program this year. I can't afford to be under the weather. We have too many projects planned."

"I've tried to tell her that it all can wait, but she won't listen," Michael said to Cassie.

"I've got too much energy to sit still for long. You ought to know that," she said, wagging her finger affectionately at her son. "And I need an answer from you. Are you going to help with the boat parade this year or not?"

"I'll help," he answered as he glanced at his watch. "But right now I have to get back to the clinic."

"You're not going to stay for lunch?"

"Can't. I have appointments scheduled. Is there anything you need before I leave?" he asked, his inquisitive glance moving from Tessie to Cassie.

Tessie waved him off with a flap of her hand. "I'm fine. I don't need to be baby-sat, you know."

"I do know that, but I'm still going to show Cassie where your medications are. So you sit tight and let me have my peace of mind," he ordered in a stern voice that was laced with affection.

"All right, Michael," she said in a timid little voice, lifting her chin so that he could plant a kiss on her cheek before he left.

He motioned Cassie to follow him inside. "She thinks she's a lot stronger than she really is," he told her when they were in the kitchen.

"She *is* going to be all right, isn't she?"

"She does have an irregular heartbeat, but the doctors say lots of people do and it's something that can be controlled by medication. Unfortunately, she hates taking drugs of any sort." He proceeded to show her where her prescriptions were and what should be taken when.

"You don't need to worry, Michael. I'll make sure she takes them," Cassie assured him.

"Great. I knew I could count on you."

He gave her the most remarkable smile then that she nearly lost her courage to say what needed to be said.

"She's right," he continued. "She doesn't need a baby-sitter, so don't feel that you have to stay until I get back. Feel free to leave whenever."

"You're coming back?"

"As soon as I've finished for the day at the clinic. So, if you don't have any other questions..." He looked at her expectantly.

"I do—I mean I don't have any other questions about Tessie, but I do think that we should talk."

He looked surprised—pleasantly so—and she could see by the way his eyes lit that he thought he was going to like what she had to say. Which only made it all the more difficult for her to begin.

"It's about the flowers," she said.

"The flowers," he repeated with an inquisitive look on his face. "Oh, you're concerned that you need to water them. Don't be. I'm sure the Mums are taking care of Tessie's garden. A couple of them show up every day."

"No, not those flowers. The roses. You know, the ones from the florist."

He gave her a blank look of bemusement.

"The coral roses," she added, wishing he didn't look as if he didn't have a clue as to what she was talking about.

"I'm afraid I'm not following you," he admitted with a half grin.

"You sent coral roses to my house," she reminded him, shifting uneasily from foot to foot.

"I did?"

"Didn't you?" she asked, although she could tell by the look on his face that he hadn't. "But the card said 'Dr. Mac.'"

"Let me get this straight. You received roses with a card saying they were from me?" When she nodded, he asked, "What else did it say?"

"For Cassandra, in case you're having a 'not so nice' day," she repeated the message that she knew by heart. Although she hadn't wanted him to send her flowers, she hadn't been able to forget the message. She'd been touched by his thoughtful gesture, or what she thought had been his thoughtfulness.

"They were the words I used that day in the hospital, when you brought your mother the roses." As soon as she said the words, she had the same awakening as he did.

"Mother." He shook his head in disbelief, a smile of chagrin on his face. "I had a hunch something like this would happen. She's never been subtle when it comes to her matchmaking attempts. I'm sorry. It's not your fault," he began, but she interrupted him.

"Please, don't make it any worse," she said, aware that her skin tone had gone from fair to blush in the space of a few minutes. "It's a bit of a relief, actually, to know that the flowers weren't from you. I mean, it would have been awkward had you sent them, since we've already established our relationship as professional, not personal."

His face sobered. "Right. We wouldn't want to cross that line, would we?"

"No," she agreed. "There's something I should have told her before now." She took a deep breath and said, "I'm not a client of the dating service. Claudia Dixon is a friend of mine. I only go to the dinners when she needs someone to fill a chair." She didn't tell him that she was paid to keep the conversation going between the guests.

His eyes narrowed. "So you weren't there looking for a date."

She shook her head. "I'm not interested in dating anyone, as I've told your mother."

"That wouldn't stop her," he said on a sardonic chuckle. "I don't think she realizes how embarrassing this can be. I'll have a talk with her."

"No." She held up her hands. "Don't. It really would make my job much easier if we just pretended it didn't happen."

"She's probably going to continue throwing us together, dropping not so subtle hints, extolling my virtues,'' he warned.

''She's already done that,'' she informed him. ''But as long as we both understand what's going on, it's not really a problem, is it?''

He didn't look convinced, but said, ''Then I won't say anything.''

''Thank you. Now I'd better get to work,'' she told him, and made her escape from the kitchen as fast as she could.

MICHAEL SOON LEARNED that it wasn't only his mother who was attempting to be a matchmaker. He made the discovery when Betty Jean asked him to stop over because her teacup poodle Peaches hadn't been feeling well all weekend. When he arrived, he discovered Cassie sitting in her kitchen helping design a poster for the garden club's annual flower sale for charity.

Betty Jean had made sure he stayed for coffee and cake, pushing his chair as close to Cassie's as possible. And when the Mum had received a phone call during their coffee break, a smile of delight had lit her features as she excused herself to take it in the other room. It came as no surprise to either him or Cassie that the phone call was a long one.

Michael expected that the matchmaking attempts would continue until Tessie's portrait was finished. Just when he thought he might have to talk to his mother and put an end to the embarrassment, three of the Mums paid him a visit and changed his mind.

They marched into his office at the clinic with long faces. Despite the smiles and the cheery greetings, he knew something was wrong.

"Ladies, what can I do for you?" he asked when they were all seated.

"This isn't a professional call, Michael," Betty Jean began.

"I didn't think it was. I don't see any animals."

"The animals are all fine," Betty Jean said curtly.

"Something obviously isn't fine. You look very serious."

Edith's sigh sounded more like a trill. "We're worried about your mother."

So that was it. Concern for his mother had prompted this visit. "She's doing fine," he assured them. "The doctors say she's in great health."

"So they told you," Francine said with an ominous ring to her voice. "We're not so sure."

"Why is that?" he asked.

"She's putting her things in order," Edith replied.

"Mother has always liked getting rid of clutter," he reminded them.

They cast furtive glances among the three of them. Then Edith leaned forward, her gloved hand on the edge of his desk. "Did you know she gave Agnes her Waterford candy dish?"

"And that beautiful paperweight she bought in France—you know, the one with the butterfly inside—that's now on Bea's desk," Francine added.

"Michael, when you reach our age, sometimes you just know when it's time to start giving things away," Betty Jean told him.

He looked at the three wrinkled faces, even more lined with worry, and searched for the right words to comfort them. "If Mom is giving things away, it's because she's discovered she has too many mementos lying around. Trust me. She just received a clean bill of health from the doctor."

They didn't look convinced. "We've heard that one before," Edith drawled sarcastically.

"Look, I know you're concerned about Mom. It's scary for anyone to be taken to the hospital in an ambulance, but I don't want you to worry about her, because she's going to be fine."

Again they exchanged glances, the looks on their faces saying they knew something he didn't. "She is eighty-one, Michael," Betty Jean reminded him

"It's not her physical health that has us concerned," Francine added. "You must have noticed that she doesn't have the joie de vivre she's always possessed?"

As much as he didn't want to admit it, he had noticed that Tessie's eyes had lost their sparkle. Although she pretended to be her usual self whenever he was around, he knew the Mums were right.

"*Is* something bothering her that I don't know about?" he asked.

Again the three of them exchanged looks, as if silently communicating who was going to be the one to answer his question. Finally Betty Jean said, "We know, but we promised your mother that we wouldn't say anything to you about it."

He leaned forward. "I appreciate your loyalty to my mother, but if there's something I could do to help her, I want to do it."

Again they exchanged glances among the three of them. "But we can't betray a confidence, Michael," Edith answered for the group.

He nearly groaned in frustration. "Well, maybe

you could give me a hint as to what I could do that would help the situation.''

Before they could answer, there was a knock on the door and Tabitha stuck her head inside. ''Sorry to interrupt, but we need you right away,'' she told Michael.

''Oh! Time for us to go,'' Francine announced as the three of them jumped to their feet.

''But you haven't told me what it is I can do for Tessie,'' he said as they headed for the door. Both Francine and Betty Jean had already hurried out of the room.

Michael put a hand on Edith's shoulder. ''You know I'd do anything I can for my mother.''

She wiggled her finger at him, motioning for him to stoop so she could whisper in his ear. ''Then find a girl and fall in love.''

INSTEAD OF GOING HOME that evening after work, Michael went to the lake, hoping he'd run into Cassie. He'd wanted to dismiss what the Mums had told him as nonsense, but the truth was he'd noticed a change in his mother's mental state lately.

He'd initially thought it was because she'd had to face her mortality. The ride in the ambulance, the stay in CICU and the diagnosis of cardiac arrhythmia to someone who'd been the picture of health her entire life—was it any wonder she'd lost a bit of the sparkle in her eyes?

Yet he also knew that long before that day, she'd been talking to him about the joys of finding that special someone. He knew that one of her greatest concerns about aging wasn't that she was getting old, but that she was getting closer to the end of her life, which meant he would be alone.

Ever since he could remember he'd told her he was never going to get married. When he was younger, she'd pooh-pooh his statement and say, "You just haven't met the right girl, that's all." Now she was convinced that he didn't have the opportunity, hence the reason for the Dinner Date gift.

As much as he hated to admit it, he knew the one thing that would make her truly happy would be for him to tell her he'd found that special someone. He knew the Mums were right. If he were to walk in her front door and tell her he was in love and planning to get married, she'd dance around the kitchen as if she'd never had a care in the world.

The problem was, he wasn't interested in finding that kind of love.

He didn't want to be crazy in love with anyone. Nor did he want a love so strong he'd be willing to die for it. Maybe love could be grand, but it could also be destructive. Tessie knew that. She'd seen what it had done to his parents, yet she continued to romanticize love and marriage.

So what did he do? He didn't want to see his mother slide slowly into a geriatric depression, yet how could he rush into a marriage with someone he barely knew just to make sure his mother was happy?

As he pulled into the Lake Minnetonka driveway, he saw Cassie's car parked in front of the house. When he walked into Tessie's kitchen, she was at the stove cooking.

"Is Mom okay?" Michael automatically asked.

"She's fine. She's in the living room watching the

Wheel,'' Cassie answered. "I'm making her dinner."
She looked nervous.

"I can see that. Smells good," he said, sniffing
appreciatively.

"It's just some pasta and chicken I threw together.
There's enough for three if you're hungry."

Just then Tessie came into the room. "I thought I
heard your voice," she said to Michael, giving him a
welcoming hug. "Isn't this a nice surprise? Have you
eaten dinner?"

"I told him there's plenty if he wants to stay,"
Cassie interjected.

"Of course he wants to stay," Tessie said, urging
him onto a chair at the table. "I'll set another place."

"You go back and finish watching the *Wheel,*" Michael told her. "I can set my own place. Besides, I
want to talk to Cassie."

If he had any doubt about her hopes that he would
be attracted to the artist, they were certainly dispelled
by the look on her face his words produced. "All
right," she said with a sugary sweet smile.

The eyes sparkled even brighter when Cassie
added, "Don't worry, Tessie. I'll take good care of
him."

As soon as they were alone he asked, "She's still
at it, isn't she?"

"At what?"

"Trying to make something happen between us."

She didn't look at him, but stirred a pot of red
sauce on the stove. "As I said before, there's no
harm. If it makes her happy…"

"You don't mind pretending that you can tolerate
my presence?"

She turned and looked at him over her shoulder. "I don't dislike you, Michael."

"Then call me Mac. That's what my friends call me."

"All right, Mac." She turned her attention again to the stove. "And to be perfectly honest I don't see anything wrong with a little bit of pretense if it means making someone as sweet as your mother happy."

"I'm glad you said that because there's something I want to ask you."

"I'LL HAVE A SLICE of the fresh strawberry," Cassie told the pie shop waitress. "And a glass of iced tea."

"Make mine lemon meringue and I'll have coffee," Michael gave his order with a smile that had the young woman lingering a few moments longer than was necessary.

Not that it should have surprised Cassie. His smile had that effect on women. It made them want to hang around and listen to what he had to say.

"Thank you for coming here with me," he said to Cassie as soon as the waitress had taken the menus and gone.

She looked at him. "Shouldn't I be thanking you? Having a piece of pie is not exactly an inconvenience."

"Maybe not, but then cooking dinner doesn't come under the job description of artist, either."

Cassie should have known that his invitation wasn't a personal one. It wasn't until he'd seen her cooking in the kitchen that he'd asked her to go out for dessert. Had he just realized that she was spending more time doing other things for his mother than sketching her?

"I thought you invited me here because you wanted to talk to me, not reward me for cooking a meal for your mother."

"I know you've been doing more than cooking for her. She told me you went to the grocery store for her, too."

She shrugged. "I had to go out for something anyway. If you brought me here to discuss hiring me to act as a companion to Tessie, I should tell you right now that, as much as I enjoy your mother's company, I'm not the person for the job."

"I don't think she needs a companion. I have another business proposition for you."

His gaze was so intent that she felt like squirming. Whatever it was he had to say, it was obvious he took it very seriously. "What kind of a proposition?" she asked.

He didn't answer immediately, and Cassie saw a small pulse throbbing at his temple. It hardly seemed possible that he was nervous, yet he lacked his usual self-confidence.

"Tell me something," he began. "How does Tessie seem to you?"

Cassie shrugged. "Fine. You did say all the tests were negative, right?"

He nodded. "Oh, yeah. Physically, she's in great shape."

The way he emphasized "physically" told her he was worried about her mental health. "But you're concerned about her emotional health?"

"Ever since her hospital stay, she hasn't been herself—at least, it seems like that to me. She acts as if she's feeling fine and tries her best to pretend that nothing's wrong, but she's not the same old Tessie."

"Mmm. I know what you mean," Cassie agreed.

"You noticed it, too?"

"I don't think she's depressed, but it's as if she has something heavy weighing on her mind."

"That's what I was afraid of," he said, leaning back against the upholstered booth in a gesture of resignation.

Just then the waitress arrived with their beverages, chatting with Michael as she poured him a cup of coffee.

As soon as she was gone, Cassie said, "It sounds as if you know what's bothering your mother."

He took a sip of coffee, then leaned forward and rested his arms on the table so that his face was closer to hers. Cassie hadn't been this close to him since the night of the Dinner Date event. She could see tiny gold flecks in his brown eyes, eyes that beckoned her to listen.

"I think I'm responsible for her mood."

"You? I don't understand."

Again his eyes pierced her with an intensity that made her feel as if he were speaking to her soul. "There's a reason why the Mums have been doing their best to throw the two of us together."

"You think your mother asked them to do it?"

He nodded, then went on to explain how three of his mother's garden club friends had come to the clinic to express their concern with Tessie's state of mind. "After all of that dancing around the issue, Edith finally told me what was bothering Mom."

She looked at him expectantly, waiting for him to tell her.

"She's afraid that when her time comes, I'll still be single and she hates the thought of leaving me alone. I'm afraid she thinks that if I'm not married, I'll end up a crusty old man with no life.''

''I think the Mums may be right,'' she told him.

''Has Tessie said the same thing to you?''

Cassie shook her head. ''No, but I overheard her talking to Louella one day and she was saying how it breaks her heart to think of you being alone. She's very protective of you and she's a firm believer in marriage. Actually, she's quite a romantic.''

His eyes softened. ''I know. She's always been like that. That's why I hate to see her worrying needlessly about something like this. I wish there was a way I could convince her that I like being single.''

''If you haven't been able to do that by now, it's probably not going to happen,'' she stated realistically.

''You may be right. After eighty-one years of believing it's love that makes the world go round, she's not going to change,'' he agreed. ''She thinks everyone's looking for that special someone.''

''But you aren't.'' She couldn't keep the skepticism from her voice.

''No, I'm not.'' He denied, then paused to look at her over the rim of his cup. ''Oh, I get it. You think because I went to the Dinner Date thing that I'm looking for a mate.''

She raised both brows. ''It would be a natural assumption, don't you think?''

He chuckled. ''Yeah, if I had been there of my own free will.''

''You weren't?''

He took a sip of coffee before answering. ''The only reason I was at the dinner was because Tessie gave it to me for a birthday present. She signed me up thinking it was the perfect gift for a thirty-five-year-old bachelor.''

''Who she wants to see married and settled down,'' she concluded. Suddenly her initial impression of him at the dinner made sense. ''So that's why you ordered Scotch. You didn't know it was a teetotalers dinner, did you?''

He smiled at the shared memory. ''Nurse Sharon informed me of the error of my ways.''

''I thought you looked a little uncomfortable during dinner,'' she said with a wry smile.

''I almost stood up and announced the reason why I was there. Except I thought I'd look even more ridiculous if I said, 'I'm only here because my mother made me come.'''

She laughed. ''You don't strike me as the kind of man who lets anyone bully him into doing anything.''

''You know Tessie. She doesn't have to bully to get her way,'' he said with great affection.

''No, that's true. She's a dear and I think it's sweet of you to suffer through a dating service dinner for your mother's sake,'' she said sincerely.

He looked her squarely in the eyes and said, ''I enjoyed that evening—especially dessert.''

Cassie was relieved that the waitress chose that moment to bring the pies to their table. She looked down at the strawberries topped with whipped cream, grateful for the diversion. The look that had been in Michael's eyes had triggered a response in her she didn't want to acknowledge.

Fortunately the young waitress again lingered, making small talk with Michael. By the time she was gone, the sexual tension of only a few moment ago had been broken.

Before taking a bite of his pie, Michael said, "So you now understand what my problem is. I need to find a way to convince my mother that she doesn't need to find me a wife."

"I'm not sure there is a way. She has her heart set on you finding the love of your life. And to be honest, Mac, I don't think she's going to stop looking until she finds it for you," Cassie answered candidly.

"Which brings us to my business proposition and where you come in."

A strawberry nearly lodged itself in her throat. She took a sip of tea to wash it down, then said, "I don't think I'm following you."

He set his fork down and clasped his hands together. "Ever since I hired you to do Tessie's portrait, you've made it perfectly clear that ours is a business relationship. Yet tonight you were very friendly during dinner. I'd say you were almost flirtatious," he said with a curious glint in his eye.

She could feel the color warm her cheeks. "I've already told you I thought it was time that we were a bit more cordial to each other, for Tessie's sake."

"I was hoping you'd say that."

"Is that what this is about? You want to bury the hatchet and put on a friendly front for your mother's sake?"

"Would it be so hard?" he asked, again those eyes causing her insides to dance to a tune she didn't want to hear.

She shrugged. "Not really. It's what we've done when the Mums have arranged for the two of us to be together, isn't it?"

"Exactly. We've pretended to enjoy each other's company." He put the emphasis on "pretended," then added, "I don't have any problem with pretense if it's harmless and for a good cause. What about you?"

"In this case the good cause being your mother's emotional health?" When he nodded, she said, "No, I don't see a problem with it."

Satisfaction gleamed in his eye. "Good."

"Is that your business proposition? You want us to act as if we enjoy each other's company when we're with your mother?"

"Actually, I think we need to pretend it's a little more than being friendly."

Her heart started to pound faster. "Are you saying you want me to pretend to be your girlfriend?"

"No, I want you to pretend to be my wife."

Chapter Eight

"You're joking, right?" Cassie thought her heart had moved into her throat.

"No." The look on his face said he was very serious.

"I can't *pretend* to be someone's wife!" The words came out a frantic whisper. "It's not right." She reached for her purse. "I'm going to go now and forget we even had this conversation."

His hand came across the table to stop her, resting on her forearm. "Please, will you just think about it for a few minutes before dismissing it as ridiculous?"

"It is ridiculous," she told him, her body trembling with emotion. He noticed and released her.

"I'm sorry. I didn't mean to upset you. I'm not doing this for me. If I wasn't so worried about my mother, I'd never consider such an idea, either. Do you know how much I hate the thought of her being distressed over something so unimportant as my love life?" His voice rose in frustration.

When he noticed her shifting uncomfortably, he lowered his voice and said, "This is the one thing I am convinced would put her mind at rest."

Cassie didn't question his motives. She'd known

Tessie long enough to know that her relationship with
her son was an extraordinary one. If there was anything that had changed her opinion of Michael in the
past few weeks, it was the respect he had for his
mother. She knew he would do practically anything
to make her happy, but *pretend to be married?*

"I'm sorry, but it just seems too dishonest," she
told him, her legs itching to get up and out of the pie
shop. But something stopped her. Maybe it was because she knew what he said about Tessie was true.
She *was* distressed about his single status.

"A few minutes ago you admitted to me that the
reason you flirted with me at dinner tonight was for
Tessie's sake," he reminded her.

She could feel her skin flush. She'd only been par-
tially truthful when she'd said it had been for Tessie's
benefit. As much as she hated to admit it, she'd enjoyed flirting with him. Actually, she was discovering
that she enjoyed quite a few things about Michael
McFerrin.

"And didn't you say that sometimes a little pretense is good?" he continued to try to persuade her.

"A fake marriage is not a *little* pretense," she said
dryly.

"I didn't say I wanted it to be fake," he said quietly.

Cassie's mouth went so dry she could barely get
her next words out. "You just said you wanted me
to pretend to be your wife."

"Yes, pretend to love me. The marriage itself
would have to be real. I guess it would be what they
call a marriage of convenience. Real in terms of the
law, but fake in terms of emotions," he answered.

She held up her hands. "Wait a minute. I have no desire to get married again."

"I understand that. That's what makes this the ideal situation," he said, his eyes brightening with enthusiasm. "Cassie, I don't want to be married any more than you do. Don't you see? We're the perfect candidates for this type of situation. Neither of us has any illusions about why we're getting married."

"But we're *not* getting married," she told him, although she didn't understand why her legs wouldn't listen to her brain and take her out of the pie shop before she heard any more of this nonsense.

"Look at it this way," he explained. "Think of it as a contract. I'm hiring you to do a job for me. That job involves treating me as if I were your husband and pretending to be a wife in a normal marriage. The good news is that the only time you have to work at this job is when you're with my mother."

He made it sound as if it were as easy as applying for a position at his clinic.

"Other than having a piece of paper that's a binding legal document, it'll be nothing at all like a real marriage. And the only time we'll have to do any pretending is when we're around my mother."

She continued to shake her head. "It won't work. She's a smart woman. She'll guess that there's something going on."

"No, she won't. She'll only see what she wants to see. Two people who look at each other as if they've discovered some magical, crazy kind of love." His voice was convincing as he said, "It'll be a business arrangement."

She chewed on her lower lip, wondering how she could possibly even be considering such an idea. He took her silence to mean that she *was* considering it and pressed on.

"We'd make everything perfectly legal. There would be a prenuptial agreement that would spell out all the terms. Since I'm the one asking you to make the compromise of moving in with me, I'm willing to compensate you financially."

"You want to pay me to do this?"

"Yes." He quoted a monthly stipend that nearly had her jaw dropping open. "Wouldn't you like to be able to give up your day job and focus totally on your art?"

Of course she would. It was her dream, and by now she would have been doing that if Darryl hadn't left her so far in debt. It seemed rather ironic that the reason she had promised herself she'd never marry again was the very reason that tempted her to do just that.

"We can let our lawyers iron out that part of the agreement. All I ask of you is that you let my mother believe that you are in love with me and that she doesn't need to worry about me ever being alone."

"Ever? You sound as if you expect this to be a permanent arrangement."

"Tessie's not going to live forever, Cassie," he said soberly.

"But what if in the meantime you meet someone."

"We'll be able to carry on with our private lives as long as we're discreet. I don't expect you to give up your personal life, although I don't think you should be spending your time at the Dinner Date parties."

She could only stare at him dumbfounded. It all seemed surreal—sitting here in this noisy pie shop, with people talking all around them, while he casually asked her to become his wife as if he were commissioning her to do another portrait.

"We can address everything in writing. The prenuptial agreement will protect whatever concerns you have."

"Do you honestly think we'll be able to fool people? I mean, you have friends, I have friends."

"As long as my mother and her friends don't know the truth, it doesn't matter what you tell people. However, since she does have quite a large circle of friends—and we both know how fast news can travel even in a metropolitan area the size of this one—it might be wise not to tell anyone the truth except our attorneys."

"I...I don't know," she said, rubbing her temple with her fingertips.

"You don't have to make a decision right now," he told her.

She wished she could. She'd like to be able to tell him no, that in no uncertain terms was she interested in any such legal arrangement. But he'd dangled a carrot beneath her nose. The opportunity to work full-time at her art. She could kiss the temporary service goodbye.

"You said you'd want me to move in with you. What about my art studio? If I move out of my apartment, I lose that space."

He shrugged. "You can rent a studio, can't you?"

"I'll have to think about it," she said, wishing he didn't have the answers to her questions. "I'd feel more inclined to consider this arrangement if I could keep my own apartment."

"Then it wouldn't appear to the outside world that we had a normal marriage, would it?"

"No, but I'm used to having my own space."

"So am I. And I told you I have two bedrooms. One for me. One for you."

Just then the waitress stopped back with the check. "Oh—is there something wrong with the pie?" she asked Cassie, who had taken but a couple of bites and pushed it aside.

"No, it's fine. I'm just not as hungry as I thought," she said with a polite smile.

When the waitress had once again disappeared and they were alone, Michael said, "If I had known my business proposition would cause you to lose your appetite for pie, I would have waited until you were finished eating before discussing it."

Cassie noticed that he'd eaten every last bite of his piece of lemon meringue. "Yes, well, it's not every day I'm asked to get married to a man I hardly know."

"It would not be a real marriage, Cassie," he reminded her.

"Yes, it would. It's real in that it would be legal and it would be real in Tessie's eyes." She reached for her purse and this time he didn't stop her. "It's late. I'm going to go home."

He left a generous tip, then followed her to the exit. When he stopped to pay the bill at the cashier's counter, she was tempted to keep right on walking out the door, but she knew there was no point in running away from him.

He walked her to her minivan and waited as she fumbled with the keys to unlock her door. "I should have told you earlier,'' he said. ''You're a good cook.''

Cassie hated the tiny thrill of pleasure his compliment produced. She should have been her usual gracious self and said thank you, but she wasn't in her usual mood. Instead she found herself asking, ''Will that be one of my *wifely* duties—should I accept this mission?''

He finally took the keys from her and unlocked the van for her. Then he held the door open so she could slide into the driver's side. This time she did find her manners. ''Thank you.''

Before closing the door, he leaned over and said, ''Unless my mother's around, you won't have to even speak to me if you don't want to. Go home and think about what I've said and I'll call you later in the week.''

''I'll need more than a few days,'' she retorted.

''Fine. Take until next Tuesday,'' he said. ''I'll follow you to make sure you get home safely.'' With those parting words he slammed the door shut and walked away.

She opened the door and stuck her head out. ''I don't need you to follow me home. I can take care of myself.''

He simply called back, ''Good for you,'' and waved.

Cassie's hands shook as she tried to insert the key in the ignition. Finally she got the minivan started and backed out of the parking place. As she pulled onto the highway, she glanced in her rearview mirror and saw that he was right behind her.

When she hit the interstate he was still following her. Tessie had told her his practice was on the southwest edge of the Twin Cities, which meant he should have kept going straight on the freeway when she exited at St. Louis Park.

He didn't. He followed her, parking outside her apartment complex when she pulled into its parking lot. He sat there watching her as she climbed out of the minivan and up the steps to her building. It wasn't until she was safely inside the secured entry that she saw him pull away from the curb.

CLAUDIA THOUGHT CASSIE WAS joking when she told her she had received a marriage proposal. "What? Did one of my clients fall madly in love at first sight and propose to you over dessert?"

"Not exactly. And that reminds me, why didn't you tell me Dr. Mac's mother was the one who arranged for him to go to that dinner?"

'It's Michael McFerrin who proposed to you?" Claudia nearly choked on her green tea. "When did this happen?"

"A couple of days ago." She went on to explain Mac's proposition, surprised at how calm she was this morning. For two days she'd thought of hardly anything else. Unable to work, she'd finally called Claudia.

"I thought I should talk to you about it since you are not only my best friend, but my attorney," she added.

"Yes, I am, and, as both, I'm telling you that you're nuts if you go through with something like this. Why would you even contemplate such an arrangement?"

"Because it would mean I could quit working for the temp service, for one thing," Cassie answered, noticing that Degas was perched on the window ledge, purring contentedly.

"You're doing this for money?" Claudia made no secret of just how awful she thought that was. "Find another job if you must, but don't get married."

"I thought you of all people would understand. You make a living arranging marriages," Cassie pointed out to her.

"Correction. I make a living bringing people together to have dinner. I don't advise anyone to marry for convenience's sake," Claudia corrected her, reaching for one of the cookies Cassie had arranged on a small china plate.

"Well, I married for love the first time and look where that got me," she said bitterly.

"So this time around you're going to ignore the basic ingredient of a good marriage?"

"If you're talking about love, as far as I'm concerned, it's not what makes a marriage good." She didn't care that she sounded cynical. This was Claudia, her best friend, who understood her.

"Don't tell me you're seriously considering this offer?" When Cassie didn't respond right away, she dropped the cookie and said, "Oh, my gosh, you are!" She slid across the couch, placed her hands on Cassie's shoulders and gave a little shake. "Who are you and what have you done with my friend Cassie?"

Cassie smiled. "All right, you've made your point."

Claudia leaned back against the sofa cushions and exhaled a sigh of relief. "Thank goodness. You had me scared there for a moment."

"I didn't say you'd *won* your point."

"You did ask me to come over here," Claudia reminded her.

"Because I do need your advice." She went over to the desk to retrieve a legal-size tablet. She plopped it down on the coffee table in front of her friend. "Look. I've made a list of what I think should be the legal concerns I have. See what you think."

Reluctantly Claudia took a look at the list. When she'd finished going over each point with Cassie, she said, "I noticed there's nothing as to how long this marriage will last. Don't you think you should provide yourself with an escape clause?"

"Do I need one?"

"Yes." She took a pen and scribbled on the notepad. "It should be worded something like this, but if you're determined to go through with this idea, it's better if I meet with his lawyer to draft an acceptable prenuptial agreement."

"All right. *If* I decide to accept this *business* arrangement, I'll make sure you see the contract before I sign anything. Fair enough?"

"Fair enough."

Cassie reached for her teacup and took another sip. "Besides the obvious financial benefits, it would be nice to be able to hide behind the shield of a wedding ring. I'm tired of men hitting on me."

"And you think a wedding ring will change that? Good grief, girl. Look in the mirror!"

"All right, so it won't eliminate all of it, but at least I won't feel like a pound of flesh on the market. And it's not like I won't have everything spelled out in print beforehand."

"You know, it's all fine and dandy to make sure your legal rights are protected, but there is no way you can draw up an agreement that will protect the rights of your heart.''

"Didn't you hear what I said? This is going to be a marriage of convenience. My heart isn't involved.''

"Maybe not now.'' She eyed Cassie curiously. "People become more attractive as you get to know them.''

"You've forgotten. I'm immune to a handsome face,'' she retorted. "I have Darryl to thank for that.''

"That's what's worrying me.''

Cassie frowned. "Why? I would think that would give you peace of mind. Thanks to Darryl, I will never make the mistake of trusting a man simply because he makes my heart go pitter-patter.''

"Does Mac McFerrin do that for you?''

She needed to look away so that her best friend wouldn't see in her face what she was trying so very hard to conceal. She reached for the teapot to pour herself another cup. "It would be silly of me to say he's not good-looking, wouldn't it?''

"That's not what I asked.''

Cassie hated the fact that her teacup rattled against the saucer when she lifted it from the table. "He has the same attitude toward marriage as I do. He wants nothing to do with it.''

That produced a sardonic laugh from Claudia. "Then why are the two of you getting married?''

Cassie looked at her then. "Because this is a way to be married but not be married. Don't you see? It'll eliminate the problems we've both faced as singles.''

"What problems?''

"Well, for one, the inconvenience of always having your friends want to set you up with another one of their single friends. You know the reason I have no social life outside of Dinner Date is because I got tired of arriving at someone's house and discovering a single guy seated next to me.''

''If you marry this guy, you're always going to have a man seated next to you,'' Claudia reminded her. ''It comes with the wedding ring. He'll be there at dinner, at breakfast and at lunch. In the car, at the store, when you want to get away with your girl-friends.''

''Uh-uh. This is different than a regular marriage. We've agreed to live separate lives. It's only when we're with his mother that we need to pretend to be a couple,'' she explained.

''Do you honestly think you can do that? Pretend to be happily married?''

''I wouldn't agree to it if I didn't think I could.''

Claudia raised her brows. ''Well, you *are* good at pretending to enjoy other people's company. I've seen you do that at Dinner Date. I suppose you could take it a step further and pretend to be madly in love. You do have the art of flirting down to a science.''

''Yes, and so many of those men I flirt with at Dinner Date are boring. At least Mac is an interesting man,'' she remarked.

''I just hope he's not too interesting,'' Claudia said on a note that sounded rather ominous.

Cassie took a sip of her tea, then set her cup down. ''What? You think I'm going to fall for the guy?''

''You never did answer my question. *Does* he make your heart go pitter-patter?''

''No,'' she lied, then quickly changed the subject when she noticed Claudia's cup was empty. ''We're out of tea. Should I make us more or do you have to leave?''

"As much as I'd like to stay and discuss this further, I have an appointment at three." Claudia rose to her feet.

Cassie followed her to the door. "Thanks for coming over and helping me with this."

"You asked for my professional opinion and you got it. Now, the question is, are you going to take my advice?" Claudia asked, as she paused with her hand on the doorknob.

"You don't think I should go through with it, do you?" Cassie didn't need to ask the question. She already knew the answer.

"Are you going to?"

"Probably." She threw her hands up in the air in a gesture of frustration. "Oh, I don't know. Maybe I'm crazy to even consider something like this."

"You don't need to make a decision today, do you?"

"No, but I want this resolved," she said.

"As your friend I'm saying please don't rush this decision. Think it through very carefully, but I want you to know that no matter what you decide, I'm a damn good lawyer. I'll make sure you're protected legally."

Cassie gave her a hug. "Thanks. I appreciate that."

But it wasn't the protection of her legal rights that was on Cassie's mind the rest of the afternoon. It was Dr. Mac. The thought of moving into his apartment with him, living under the same roof, pretending to be in love whenever they were in Tessie's presence sent funny shivers of anticipation through her.

Not long after Claudia had gone, she called Mac at the clinic.

"Hi. It's Cassie. Could we meet somewhere? I've reached a decision."

As Cassie sat on a bench outside the fenced area known as Monkey Island waiting for Mac to arrive, she didn't know which was more fascinating—the monkeys, or the people trying to get their attention. She watched both, amused by human antics which she discovered the monkeys often mimicked.

"Having fun?"

The voice came from her left. She shielded her eyes from the sun and looked up to see Mac standing next to her bench. He wore a pair of faded denims and a white T-shirt. On his head was a navy blue baseball cap with a red M appliquéd across the front.

"This is a pretty good spot for people watching," Cassie answered, trying not to notice the way the T-shirt hugged his chest. She slid over and patted the bench. "Want to sit?"

He took her up on her offer, sitting down beside her. As he did, she caught the scent of the men's fragrance that was becoming familiar to her. It was woodsy smelling and tickled her nerves like a fine wine tickles the palate.

"What do you think of the monkeys?"

"The ones behind the fence or the ones outside?" she asked with an impish grin that had him smiling. He looked so relaxed she didn't want to have to bring up the subject of why they were there.

"Ever since I was a kid, this has been one of my favorite places to come. Tessie would pack us a picnic lunch and we'd make a day of it. Eat in the park, rent a paddleboat over at the lake, then come back here to look at the animals, and of course, ride the rides."

"I don't remember there being amusement rides here," she commented.

"They've been gone a while, but there used to be a small area where you could ride the tilt-a-wheel or the Ferris wheel," he reflected nostalgically. "That's right. You didn't grow up in the Twin Cities, did you?"

She shook her head.

He sat quietly for several moments, as if soaking up the smells and sights that triggered all those childhood memories. As he made a sweeping glance of the area, it was almost as if she could see the little boy in him relishing his moments at the zoo.

She would have liked to have had him show her around the rest of the animal domains, but she knew she wasn't there on a pleasure visit. She had come to give him an answer and the sooner that was done, the sooner she could get back to life as usual.

"My lawyer needs to contact your lawyer," she said.

Suddenly the little boy was gone. "Does this mean you've decided to accept my business proposition?" Any emotion there might have been on his face was masked with a blank look.

"Yes." She was surprised at how easily the affirmative rolled off her lips.

"Good. I think it'll be a mutually beneficial proposition. I get the peace of mind concerning my mother, you get the opportunity to be a full-time artist."

"Yes, that's exactly the way I look at it," she agreed.

"Then I guess we're all set." He rose to his feet, as if he were in a hurry to get away.

She jumped up, too. "What happens next?"

He looked away, as if studying the horizon. "We'll need to set a date for the wedding, but before we do that, we'd better give the Mums something to talk about. I can't propose to you without courting you first."

"No, they need to think we're dating," she agreed.

He still didn't look at her, but continued staring off in the distance. "If I stop over to my mother's while you're there and ask you out, that should get the ball rolling. And we can use the Fourth of July boat parade to show them how well suited we are to each other."

"Then you want me to be at the lake on the Fourth of July?"

He looked at her. "Weren't you planning on being there? I thought the Mums had roped you into helping organize the event."

"No. I usually spend the Fourth with some friends."

His eyes narrowed slightly. "Don't you think it would look funny if you weren't with me on the holiday?"

"It's not a problem. I can be there."

They could have been two zoo workers discussing who was going to work which schedule, so impersonal was their conversation. Suddenly Cassie heard a woman's voice call out, "Mac!"

She turned to her left to see a woman pushing a stroller coming toward them. Mac smiled and waved with one hand, his other arm snaking around Cassie's waist in a very possessive manner.

"Nancy, how's it going?" he asked the redhead as she approached. Then he turned to Cassie and said,

"Cassie, this is Nancy Larson. Nancy, Cassie Carrigan."

"It's nice to meet you," Cassie said politely as she shook the young mother's hand.

"Cassie is the artist doing my mother's portrait," Mac explained to Nancy, then to Cassie he said, "Nancy is Louella's granddaughter."

Which explained the reason for Mac's possessive stance. With his hand still resting on Cassie's waist, he made sure there was no doubt in Nancy's mind that Cassie was more than an artist doing his mother's portrait.

As the three of them exchanged pleasantries, Cassie saw what a great actor Mac could be. The intimate glances, the smiles, the slight nudges all designed to make sure Nancy didn't miss the boat.

When she and her two-year-old son had waved goodbye and were out of view, Mac said, "That was a lucky break. She's going to go home and call her grandmother. I'd bet money on it."

The wheels had been put in motion. Cassie wasn't sure whether she should be happy or horrified. "Should I mention that we ran into her when I see your mother tomorrow?"

"Mom will probably mention it to you," he said with a knowing chuckle. "Who would have thought we'd run into someone connected to the Mums at the zoo?"

She could see it was rhetorical question he didn't expect would be answered. "Do we have anything else to discuss? If not, I'd like to get home before it gets dark."

"Why don't I take you out to dinner on Saturday?"

"To discuss business?"

He nodded. "I'll have my lawyer contact your lawyer this week, but we need to work out a schedule. Iron out some of the details."

"Such as?"

"When you want to see my condo. I should probably also come over to your place and see how much furniture you have to move in."

"I thought I was keeping my apartment."

"Your studio maybe, but you're going to have to live with me."

"Why?"

"Why?" he repeated as if it were the most stupid question he'd ever heard. "What if Mom calls my place looking for you and you're not there?"

"Tell her I'm out."

"In the middle of the night?"

"Why would she call in the middle of the night?"

"You can relax. I don't expect our pretense to extend to the bedroom."

That brought a flush to her face.

He stood facing her, feet spread wide, hands on his waist. "If we're going to be convincing that this relationship is for real, we can't risk making any mistakes."

"I don't want to give up my apartment," she said a bit stubbornly. "I like sleeping in my own room in my own bed. My cat likes that, too."

He looked as if he were going to argue, but said, "Fine, but you're going to have to move some of your things to my place. My mom will come visit us."

She knew he had a point. "All right. We can move some of my things over to your place *after* we're married."

He smiled, a warm, sexy smile that did funny things to her insides. "Is seven okay for Saturday?"

"Seven will be fine," she answered.

"Good." Then to her surprise, he pulled her into his arms and kissed her. It was a short barely-there kiss, but it was long enough to make Cassie's blood race.

"Why did you do that? There's no one around," she told him.

"Just practicing," he said with a wicked smile, then turned around and was gone.

Chapter Nine

Just as Michael predicted, the Mum grapevine was at work. When Cassie arrived at Tessie's the following afternoon, she discovered its efficiency.

"And how are you today?" Tessie greeted her with her usual perky smile.

"I'm fine. Shouldn't I be asking you that question?" Cassie said as she set her sketch pad on the patio table.

"I am terrific," the senior citizen said, then did a shuffle of her feet in a dance pattern on the patio to prove it. "See. No shortness of breath, no pains in my chest. And it's a glorious day!" She spread her arms as if to gather up the air.

"It is, isn't it?" Cassie agreed, glancing out across the yard to the lake where several sailboats drifted across the bay.

"Do we have time to chat today or would you like to get started?"

"Why don't we go straight to the gazebo and when we've finished, we'll visit. I brought you something from the bakery." She handed her a small white sack.

Tessie made a sound of delight and peeked inside. "Ooh. Éclairs. How did you know I love them?"

"Actually, Michael told me."

"He did, did he?" Her eyes twinkled in merriment. "When was that? When he took you to the pie shop the other night?"

Cassie knew it was the perfect opportunity to drop a hint that she was interested in Michael. "Actually, it was yesterday. Should we get something to drink to take with us while we work?" she asked, trying to sound nonchalant about their being together.

"Why, of course," Tessie sputtered. "Come inside and you can tell me more." She motioned for Cassie to follow her into the house.

While Tessie poured them each a glass of iced tea, Cassie told her about meeting Michael at the zoo.

"What a coincidence that the two of you would run into each other like that," Tessie remarked as she gave Cassie a glass and they headed back outdoors. "I don't think Michael has been to that zoo since he was a teenager."

Cassie knew it was the opening she needed. "It's a wonderful zoo. Of course, it's much more interesting when you're with someone who knows so much about animals," she said in a tone that would leave no doubt as to how impressed she was with Tessie's son.

"Then it's a good thing you had Michael there, isn't it?"

"Yes. He's very smart—but of course I don't need to tell you that, do I?" she said as they climbed the steps to the gazebo. "Why don't you sit down and we'll get started?"

Although Tessie tried to continue their conversation, Cassie persuaded her to sit quietly until she had finished sketching. Several times during the session, however, she'd catch a squirrel in the corner of her vision and follow it as it ran toward the house.

"Are you looking for someone?" Tessie finally asked.

Recognizing another opportunity, Cassie didn't admit that it was the antics of a squirrel that had her glancing toward the house. "I thought Michael had said he was going to stop over."

"If he told you he would, then I'm sure he will," Tessie answered cheerily.

Several times during their session, Cassie paused to give Tessie a break, allowing her to move around. Each time, she would mention Michael's name, and Tessie's eyes would gleam.

When she could see the older woman was getting tired, she suggested they stop for the day. As she was putting away her sketch pad, the sound of tires on gravel alerted her to a car coming in the driveway. Cassie's heartbeat increased and she felt that crazy little trembling of excitement in her stomach.

When a horn honked, Tessie said, "I wonder if that's Michael."

Cassie's mouth went dry as she waited for him to appear. Only it wasn't Michael's tall figure that walked through the trellis of ivy into Tessie's backyard. It was Betty Jean.

The look of disappointment on Cassie's face was genuine. Tessie noticed and patted her hand. "I'm sure he's still going to come."

"Hello, hello," Betty Jean called out excitedly, waving her arm in a gesture that indicated she wanted them to join her. "I have something I want to show you!"

Cassie accompanied Tessie up the walk and

through the trellis as they followed Betty Jean around to the front of the house. Cassie thought maybe the older lady had bought a new car and wanted to show it off, but when they reached the driveway she saw Betty Jean's 1986 Grand Marquis. The front passenger door was wide-open and Betty Jean leaned inside to retrieve something from the floor.

When she straightened, she held a tiny puppy no bigger than a softball. "I finally found one." She cradled the trembling white ball of fur close to her, turning so they could get a better look. "It's a bichon-poo. Three quarters bichon, one quarter toy poodle. Isn't she precious?"

The consensus was that she was indeed the sweetest puppy ever to be born, as both Tessie and Cassie oohed and aahed over the tiny pup. Betty Jean set her down in the grass and all three women giggled as tiny legs tried to navigate through the thick carpet of grass.

"Oh, I'm so glad you brought her over here," Tessie gushed as she played with the little dog.

"It was Michael's idea. He wanted to see her," Betty Jean explained.

As if on cue, the big blue Explorer pulled into the driveway. Again Cassie's heartbeat accelerated. And she could feel her palms sweating and her mouth went dry. As he climbed out of the truck, she wished he didn't have to be so darn good-looking. For that's why her body reacted this way every time she saw him. She was, after all, only human, and he was a very attractive man.

Before he was even out of the car, Betty Jean had lifted the bichon-poo into her hands and had carried her over to the Explorer. "Here she is, Michael. Isn't she just adorable?"

"For Pete's sake, Betty Jean. Let Michael say hello to everyone," Tessie scolded lightly.

As if suddenly realizing that she was getting in the way of a matchmaking scheme, Betty Jean apologized. "Your mother's right. You should say hello to Cassie before you give little Phoebe a look."

"Hello, Cassie," he said. The look he cast in her direction was enough to make her legs go weak. If she'd had any doubt that he could put on a convincing act that he was crazy about her, it was gone now.

"Hi," she said, almost shyly. She wished he'd quit looking at her as if he wanted to undress her right there on the spot.

Tessie pulled him by the arm over to the front porch where Cassie sat on the lowest step. "If you're going to look that dog over, you'd better sit down," she ordered, and practically shoved him down next to Cassie.

Michael's knees bumped hers, both were bare. She wore a pair of khaki shorts; he wore a pair of dark green ones. He smelled like soap, as if he'd just come from a shower. It was almost as big an aphrodisiac as the fragrance he usually wore but tonight was absent.

Cupping the puppy in his large hands, he leaned over so that she could have as close a view as he did. Unfortunately, it meant that their two heads were very close together—so close, she could feel his breath on her cheek.

"What do you think? Is she a keeper?" he asked, his voice taking on an intimate quality, as if he were talking to a lover. It sent a tingling through her.

Cassie had to swallow to get rid of her dry mouth before speaking. "She's so tiny and fragile."

"She doesn't weigh much, that's for certain. Why don't you hold her while I take a closer look? Just spread your hands and make a shelf."

She did as she was told and held the tiny puppy while he examined her. After a few minutes he said to Betty Jean, "Everything seems to be normal. Why don't you call the clinic tomorrow and you can bring her in for a more thorough exam."

"She needs the next series of shots. It's on the card in my purse," she told him.

"She sure is a cute thing." Mac looked at Cassie as he said the words.

His mother and Betty Jean noticed. Cassie saw Betty Jean nudge Tessie with her elbow and exchange knowing glances.

Tessie offered to make coffee for everyone. Michael accepted the offer, but her friend insisted she needed to get home with Phoebe. By the time Betty Jean's big old Grand Marquis pulled out of the driveway, Cassie was certain that the reason she was in such a hurry wasn't because of the new puppy, but because she couldn't wait to get on the Mum grapevine.

When Tessie excused herself to go inside to put on the coffee, Cassie offered to help her, but Michael grabbed her by the hand.

"Why don't you stay out here with me?" he said with that "I want you" look in his eye he'd been casting her way all evening.

Tessie noticed it, too, and said, "Yes. You sit outside here with Michael. I'll call you in when it's ready.'' She patted her hand as if she were a small child needing reassurance, then disappeared inside.

''Alone at last,'' Michael said as he came up behind her and grabbed her around the waist. Next to her ear, he whispered, ''She's watching through the window and she can probably hear us, too. We might as well take advantage of it.''

Cassie could flirt with the best of them. She turned into his embrace, wrapping her hands around his broad shoulders. ''Did you have a good day?''

''It wasn't bad, but it's definitely improved now that you're in it.'' He planted a kiss on her lips, one that was so totally unexpected that, when it was over, she could only stare at him with her mouth open. ''For Mom's benefit,'' he whispered.

If that was what he could do when he was faking it. Cassie wondered just what it would be like to be kissed by him if he was doing it for all the right reasons. She looked away, not wanting him to see any questions that might be on her face.

''I had a wonderful time at the zoo yesterday,'' she told him when she regained her composure.

''So did I. You're an easy person to be around, Cassie.''

''So you like being around me?'' she asked provocatively.

''You know I do,'' he said, and gave her another kiss. If she had thought the first one had packed a bit of a punch, this one nearly knocked her off her feet.

With a very deliberate movement, his mouth covered hers in a long, lingering kiss that started as a surprisingly soft and sensitive exploration of her lips. It was light contact, the kind of kiss that Cassie knew she'd be able to react to mechanically, going through the motions in order to make it look to anyone watching that she was responding.

What she hadn't counted on was that the very sweetness of the kiss would be the reason her lips would part beneath his. Something that had lain dormant for many years came to life when his mouth moved over hers. With a small, needy sound, she parted her lips, and he didn't hesitate to respond to the invitation.

She'd forgotten what it was like to be kissed until nothing else mattered but the exquisite sensation of desire consuming her thoughts. To want nothing more than to have the kiss go on and on….to stop only because you were breathless.

When it ended, she was grateful that he still had his arms around her, because she wasn't sure her legs wouldn't buckle beneath her. She took advantage of the rock-solid shoulder he offered, resting her head against it while she waited for her breathing to return to normal.

If the kiss had affected him the same way, he didn't let her see it. One thing he couldn't hide, however, was the beating of his heart. She could feel it pounding beneath her palm and she was happy that he wasn't as indifferent as he wanted her to believe.

"It's such a beautiful evening. We should be out front, watching the sun set on the lake," he told her.

"That's a great idea. I'll bring the coffee out when it's ready," Tessie's voice called through the window.

"See what I mean?" he whispered.

Cassie guessed that the reason he wanted to go to the lake was so that they could drop the pretense—at least for a while. But when they reached the lake, he took her by the hand and led her to a wooden bench at the end of the dock where he sat, pulling her down beside him.

"I don't think she can hear us out here, but she can see us." His arm came up and slid around the back of the bench to rest on her shoulder.

"She must have the picture by now," Cassie said softly, wishing that sitting so close to him didn't feel so right.

"I'm sure the Mums do, too," he remarked. "I'm convinced Betty Jean only brought Phoebe over here because she wanted to see firsthand if the rumors were true. She and Louella are neighbors."

"The phone lines are probably buzzing as we speak."

"I talked to my attorney today. He said it shouldn't take more than a week or two to get the prenuptial agreement drafted," he told her.

"We probably shouldn't rush things or your mother might get suspicious," Cassie stated evenly. She was surprised at how easy it was to talk about something so serious as marriage in such a detached way.

"Are you kidding? Didn't she tell you that she met Frank on a Saturday afternoon and married him three weeks later?"

She had heard that story. Tessie had told it several times, as if wanting to make sure Cassie was aware that love could happen very quickly in a woman's life.

"They were in love."

"Which is my point. If Tessie believes we are, then she won't question us wanting to get married right away."

Married right away. He made it sound as if he was

thinking of doing it as soon as the prenuptial agreement was signed. "You sound as if you don't want to wait very long before we do make everything legal."

"There's not any point in waiting, is there?" Suddenly he lifted his arm and pointed to the neighbor's dock to their left. "Look. There's a gray heron."

Standing on one slender leg, the large bird made the perfect silhouette against the golden hue of the sky. "It's beautiful."

He didn't mention the wedding date again, but talked about the wildlife that inhabited the area. She liked listening to him, his passion for the outdoors obvious by the tone of his voice.

A short while later, as if suddenly realizing he was the one who'd been doing all the talking, he said, "I'm boring you, aren't I?"

"No, not at all."

He gave her a dubious look. Just then Tessie's voice carried across the still air as clear as if she were only a few feet from them rather standing just outside the house.

"Time to pretend again," he said, clasping her hand in his.

When they arrived at the house, Tessie had set the kitchen table with her best china and linens. Besides coffee, she'd made a pot of tea and on a plate were the éclairs Cassie had brought for her.

"Oh, you shouldn't have fussed. We could have sat outside," Cassie told her.

"I didn't fuss. And if they aren't already out now, the bugs would have soon chased us indoors," Tessie retorted. She poured Michael a cup of coffee, then turned to Cassie, "Coffee or tea?"

"I'll have some tea, thank you. Now you sit down." Cassie reached for the teapot and filled both her and Tessie's cups.

"Isn't this lovely?" Tessie could barely contain her joy. "I am so blessed to have you two here with me," she said, reaching out to touch each of their hands.

"I feel the same way," Michael told her, smiling first at his mother, then giving Cassie a look that made her whole body tingle.

"This is very nice," Cassie added, smiling provocatively at Michael. Tessie noticed but didn't comment. She simply sat there looking like the cat who'd discovered the bowl of cream.

For the first time since she'd been released from the hospital, Tessie's cheeks glowed and Cassie knew that Michael could see the difference in her spirit. As he walked her out to her minivan, he thanked her for doing such a fine job of convincing his mother that she was interested in him.

"You don't need to thank me, Michael." She discovered she was on edge and she didn't want to hear any sort of thanks or reminder of what she'd done this evening.

He didn't seem to notice anything out of the ordinary. "I'll call you when I get those papers. I probably should bring them over to your place to have you sign them."

"You can bring them—" She stopped when she realized she had almost said he could bring them to Tessie's. Of course he couldn't. "Maybe we could meet for coffee somewhere and I'll sign them then."

"I'm going to have to come over to your apartment sooner or later," he told her.

She knew what he said was true, but right now in

her head she needed to keep their arrangement strictly business. She planned to use her apartment as her sanctuary, the place she could go when she needed to be alone—when she needed to be away from him. It was important to her peace of mind that he not be a part of it.

When she hesitated, he said, "Cassie, I'm going to be your husband. I need to know where you live and you need to see my place."

She knew what he said was true. "All right. Call me when you get the papers." She didn't mean for her voice to sound so testy. She pulled the door shut, but her window remained open.

He bent, resting his arms along the window opening so that his face was only inches from her. She thought he might want to kiss her, but all he said was, "I'll follow you home."

"It's not necessary," she told him.

He simply straightened, calling out a good-night as he walked back to his Explorer. And just as he had the night they'd been at the pie shop, he drove right behind her all the way back to Minneapolis, passing up his exit on the freeway so that he could make sure she got home safely. As she used her key to unlock the secured entry of the apartment complex, she looked back and he waved, then pulled away.

As much as Cassie hated to admit it, it felt good that he was there.

"ORDER, LADIES. We must begin," Louella said with several claps of her gavel.

But it was difficult to quiet the Mums on this bright June morning.

"Ladies, please!" Louella tried again. This time,

they all took their seats at Betty Jean's table and turned their attention to the leader.

"Since I don't think we're going to get any business done until Tessie gives us a report on the courtship of Dr. Mac, I'm going to ask her to begin."

Tessie sprang to her feet. "As you all know, it worked!"

Cheers and applause echoed through the room.

"I think it was the coral roses, but I can't say for sure," Tessie continued.

"Don't forget I had Cassie come over and make those posters for us on the very day I knew Dr. Mac was stopping in," Betty Jean reminded everyone.

"And I left my scarf with the program in his truck," Violet added.

"We all worked together," Louella declared victoriously. "It probably wasn't one particular anything, but a combination of many things we did for the two of them."

Again chatter broke out among the ladies and Louella pounded the gavel. "All right. I think we all know that the courtship of Dr. Mac is a success. It's time we move on, ladies."

Edith chose that moment to stand. "Doesn't anyone want to know what really turned the tide?"

Francine quickly answered, "Edith, this is not the time to be discussing that."

"Discussing what?" Tessie wanted to know.

Francine, looking a bit nervous, said, "She's added Michael to her prayer chain."

Tessie looked at Edith. "Is that right?"

Edith stuttered, "Er…yes, I have."

"Well, thank you, dear." Tessie scooted around to the other side of the table and gave the woman a hug.

''That is so sweet of you'' Then she turned to the rest of the group and said, ''Those must have been some pretty powerful prayers.''

Edith smiled and sat down, but not before exchanging glances with Betty Jean and Francine. Tessie didn't notice.

''All right, we've taken care of Dr. Mac,'' Louella declared cheerily. ''Now let's see what we can do on our other projects.''

''OH MY. LOOK AT THIS.'' Tessie came out of the bathroom carrying a small gold band in the palm of her hand. ''It's Cassie's. She must have taken it off when she was washing up and forgot to put it back on.''

''She was here today?'' Michael asked.

Tessie nodded. ''She helped me divide the day lilies. That's why she needed to wash up. We got our hands dirty working in the garden.''

Michael discovered that the image of Cassie bent over the flower beds was a pleasant one and he smiled. He'd been doing a lot of that lately—smiling at the mention of her name.

''I'd better call her and tell her I found her ring. I don't want her to worry that she's lost it.'' Tessie reached for the phone but Michael intercepted her.

''I have a better idea. Why don't I just drop it off at her place?'' he suggested.

Tessie thought it was a wonderful idea. ''Yes, I think that's exactly what you should do.'' She handed him the small gold band and watched him examine it.

Upon closer examination Michael could see the signs of time on the narrow band. Gone was the luster and the engraving that had once been legible on the inside.

"It looks like a wedding band."

"A very *old* one," Tessie agreed.

He smiled weakly. "All right, so it's not her husband's. It's hard to believe this fits anyone," he said, amazed by how small the ring was. "She has delicate bones, doesn't she?"

"Yes, she does," his mother agreed. "She's a lovely person—and I don't just mean physically."

"I agree, Mom." He bent to give her a kiss on the cheek. "I'd better go. As you said, I'd hate to think of Cassie worrying that she's lost this." He carefully slid the ring into his pocket and headed toward the door. "Oh—and you can make that phone call now. Tell her I'm on my way."

As MICHAEL EXPECTED, Cassie was not thrilled to see him. When she opened the door, he stood with his hand raised, the ring between his thumb and forefinger.

"You didn't have to bring it all the way over here," she said, taking it from his fingertips. "I'm going back to Tessie's tomorrow."

There was no hello, no "it was nice of you come all this way."

"I thought it would be a good time for us to talk." He waited for her to invite him in. For a moment it looked as if she might not, but then she stepped aside and gestured for him to enter.

An antique hat tree with hats on every hook and a mirror in the middle stood just inside the entrance. He expected he'd find more antiques, but to his surprise her apartment had a very modern look to it. As he walked into her living room, he felt as if were walking into a black-and-white movie. There was very little color except for the art on her walls.

They weren't portraits, but landscapes—beautiful, impressionistic landscapes. He asked, "Did you do those?"

She shook her head. "No, a friend of mine did. Aren't they wonderful?"

He nodded.

"Would you like something to drink?" she asked politely.

"Ah, sure. That'd be great," he said, still looking around the room, which had a very artsy feel to it.

"Soda all right?" she asked.

"Sure."

"Have a seat and I'll be right back."

While she was gone, he continued to look around the room. A large overstuffed sofa in a dark gray, an old wooden rocker with a black leather seat that looked as if it would hold two of Cassie, a torchère steel floor lamp with a pink shade. An eclectic assortment that he would have never expected to work so well together.

What was missing he realized were photographs. He did a quick survey of all the tabletops and shelves and found none. He did find a cat. An almost chocolate colored Abysinnian sitting perfectly still on the window ledge. Only his eyes moved as he watched Michael nose around the place.

"I'm sorry, but this is all I have," Cassie said as she came into the room and handed him a glass with a bright red liquid inside. "It's strawberry."

"Strawberry's good," he said, then he chose to sit

down on a large ottoman rather than sit beside her on the sofa.

Within seconds a cat joined him, meowing in protest.

"Degas, get down," Cassie commanded.

The cat didn't move, but continued to rub up against Michael's back.

"He thinks that's his chair." With one hand she lifted the cat and deposited him on the floor. He immediately jumped back up onto the ottoman.

"It's all right," Michael told her, scratching the ears of the Abysinnian. "I'm used to sharing my space with animals."

Cassie shrugged and took a seat on the sofa. As she did, he noticed one of the sofa pillows had a saying cross-stitched across the front. It read You Can't Build A Reputation On What You Are Going To Do.

"I like your pillow," he told her.

She picked it up and looked at it, her eyes softening. "I got this when I was in art school."

"Was that before or after you were married?" he asked.

"Before," she said simply. "What did you want to talk to me about?"

He was becoming accustomed to her trying to steer the conversation away from her personal life. It was actually something he found quite fascinating about her. She was an excellent conversationalist, but he'd quickly discovered that although she talked a lot, she rarely talked about herself. He was determined to change that.

"I thought we should make sure we're prepared to the next step. Since the prenuptial agreement is done, we can announce our engagement."

"And when would you like to do that?" He could see she was pretending to be more relaxed than she actually was. The fingers around the soda glass were clenched so tightly her knuckles were turning white.

"I thought maybe the Fourth of July might be a good time."

He took her silence to be agreement and continued. "However, if we're going to pretend to be crazy in love and making that announcement, I need to know as much about you as any other prospective husband would know about his future wife."

She took a swallow of her soda, then asked, "What do you want to know?"

"How you met your husband. How long you were married," he answered.

"We grew up together. We were high school sweethearts. He wanted to be an actor so when he came to the cities, I followed him and went to art school."

"So you were married when?"

"In 1990. I was twenty. While he tried to make a name for himself, I took a job with an insurance company doing clerical work. He worked in local theater, then one day went to audition for a Hollywood movie. He got the part but before filming ever started, he was killed in an accident. A wall collapsed at a construction site he happened to be walking past." It was all said very matter-of-factly, as if she were a news anchor reporting the story on the nightly news.

"I'm sorry. It must have been very difficult for you."

She bit down on her upper lip before answering. "Yes, it was, which is why I hope we don't need to discuss this again."

"Of course not. How long ago was that, Cassie?"

"Four years."

He nodded. "I see. What about other family? I know you said they're in South Dakota."

"Only my aunt lives there. My father lives in Pennsylvania. He's in sales."

"And your mother?"

She didn't answer his questions but set her glass down on the coffee table and folded her arms across her chest. "Maybe you should tell me about your history."

"You mean Tessie hasn't told you my life story?" he asked with a sardonic chuckle.

She smiled then. "All right, so I probably know a little more about you than you do about me, but I'd like to hear the stuff that Tessie doesn't know. Am I going to find a mob of jealous women pounding on my door when they hear that I've taken you out of the dating game?"

Before he could answer, she added, "Or maybe I should ask if you plan to *be* out of the dating game?"

He stared at her then and felt a jolt. Until now, he hadn't realized just how little he'd thought about his social life. When he'd originally come up with the idea to get married for Tessie's sake, he'd thought he would continue on with his life in the city as he'd always done—with the exception that he would have to be discreet, of course.

Now, looking at the lovely picture Cassie made sitting curled up on the sofa, he realized that ever since she'd accepted his business proposition, he could only think of one woman being in his life. Her.

"Am I going to be expected to look the other way while you maintain certain friendships that most married men wouldn't be allowed to have?'' she pressed on when he didn't answer immediately.

"Maybe we should let that discussion go until there's a time when it's needed," he suggested, not wanting to reveal to her that he wasn't interested in any other women.

"Are you saying that even though this is a pretend marriage, you expect fidelity to be a real aspect?"

"Yes. The most important thing is for Tessie not to be hurt. If she were to think that either one of us were cheating on the other one, she'd be crushed."

"You're right. She would."

"Cassie, the reason I chose you for this arrangement was because my mother told me you were so very much in love with your husband that you've sworn to never love again. I figured that I wouldn't have to worry about you falling in love with another man while married to me, because your heart already belongs to another."

"You're right. I'm not interested in love," she admitted. "But what about you? What if you find someone you *do* want to share your life with?"

He shook her head. "That'll never happen."

"How can you be so sure?"

"I just am. If there's one thing I've learned in my lifetime, Cassie, it's to avoid that passionate, destructive kind of love."

"Then Michael, I'd say this arrangement should work out just fine."

"So should we set a date?"

"I'll get my calendar."

Chapter Ten

By nature Cassie was a sentimental person, but when it came to holidays, she'd had little opportunity to establish the traditions that caused most Americans to look forward to the Fourth of July. While the rest of the country attended picnics and parades, she usually spent her time working on Independence Day. It was what she had learned as a child. As a hospital nurse, her aunt had had little choice but to work holidays, which meant Cassie either tagged along with a friend to a Fourth of July celebration or she stayed home.

Not much changed when she married Darryl, except she became the adult responsible for paying part of the bills. Not that it mattered to Darryl if she worked a holiday. His idea of patriotism had been to gather up as many of his drinking buddies as he could find and have a bang-up time in the backyard setting off illegal fireworks. As unhappy as she'd been that first summer following his death, it had been a relief not to have drunken men trying to set off explosives at her feet.

So for Cassie, the Fourth of July was just another day in which the postal service didn't deliver mail and the banks were closed. Although Claudia always made sure she knew she was welcome to attend their annual barbecue should she get a craving for a hamburger off the grill, Cassie usually spent the day at home in the quiet of her apartment listening to the music of John Philip Sousa broadcast over public television.

This year she knew it would be a very different Fourth from the previous ones she'd celebrated. Not only had Tessie invited several of the Mums to the annual McFerrin picnic, she'd discovered that several of Mac's friends would be there. To Cassie it was a daunting thought, especially since she was already nervous about announcing her engagement to Mac.

True to his word, he was at her apartment bright and early on the Fourth of July morning. Along with her swimsuit, towel and sunscreen, Cassie had packed a change of clothes plus a sweatshirt just in case the air cooled significantly after sundown. Her contribution to the picnic feast was three loaves of orange bread that she'd baked the night before.

Mac said very little on the way to Lake Minnetonka. Cassie wondered if he was as apprehensive as she was about the pretense they were about undertake. He'd been very cool toward her ever since he'd arrived at her place, yet he gave no indication that he was considering changing his mind about going through the plan.

The farther away from the city they drove, the more nervous Cassie became. By the time he pulled into Tessie's driveway, her stomach felt like the inside of a washing machine going through a heavy cycle.

''I like the flags,'' she said to Michael, noticing the red-white-and-blue flags strung together between the roofs of the garage and the house, flapping gently in the breeze.

"I put them up last night. It's a tradition. Wait until you see the picnic area down by the lake. Lights everywhere, paper lanterns…more flags. Tessie's very patriotic."

At the thought of the older woman, Cassie fidgeted nervously. She closed her eyes briefly and took a deep breath, trying to calm her nerves.

Mac noticed her uneasiness. "Relax. It'll be fine."

His words did little to ease her anxiety. "Maybe I should have worn slacks instead of this skirt," she said, noticing how the cotton had already wrinkled in several places.

"You look great," he said as she tried to smooth the fabric with her fingers.

"I feel like a nervous wreck. I wish there weren't going to be so many people here," she said, unzipping the bag at her feet and pulling out a brush. She pushed it through her hair with a jerkiness that had Michael repeating himself.

"Will you please relax?"

"How can I? I'm worried I'm going to make a mistake," she admitted.

He reached across the seat and grabbed her hand. "Cassie, look at me." When she did, his eyes held hers. "You trust me, right?"

"If I didn't, I wouldn't be going through with this," she replied candidly, appreciating the strength of his hands as they held hers.

"I thought you were a woman who enjoyed a challenge as much as I do? Or was that evening with Dinner Date a pretense, too?"

"No. I may be a flirt, but I'm not a liar," she said with a lift of her chin.

He smiled then. "Good. That's what I wanted to hear. All you have to do is be yourself. Just behave the way you did that first night we met. I'll take it from there. Trust me."

When he looked at her with that penetrating gaze and spoke with that persuasive tone, she found herself wanting to do just that. "All right. I can do this," she stated with conviction.

"I know you can. Now let's go find Tessie. We have news to share with her."

Cassie felt as if it were someone else's legs carrying her into the house. She wondered if she would have made it if Mac hadn't been there to support her. However, when she saw the look on Tessie's face as they walked hand in hand into the kitchen, her stomach stopped agitating.

"Oh! Look at the two of you." Tessie stepped back and gazed at them. "You make such a handsome couple!"

Michael slipped his arm around Cassie's shoulder and gave a gentle squeeze. "I'm a lucky man to have such a beautiful woman for my Independence Day date, aren't I?" The look he gave Cassie nearly had her knees buckling.

Tessie cooed in delight, then led them into the dining room where an assortment of plastic flags of various sizes along with rolls of red, white and blue crepe paper lay scattered across the table. Clinging to the ceiling were dozens of helium-inflated balloons.

"As you can see, Cassie, our first task is to decorate the boat for the parade," Tessie explained.

"Actually, Mother, before we do that, Cassie and

I have something we want to tell you,'' he said, pulling Cassie even more tightly to him.

Tessie looked expectantly from one to the other.

His voice was perfectly calm as he said, ''I know this might seem rather sudden, but I've asked Cassie to be my wife, and she's said yes.''

''Oh!'' Tessie covered her mouth with both hands, her eyes widening in disbelief. Then she placed a hand over her heart and tears pooled in her eyes. ''Oh, my goodness. I don't think I've ever been so happy in my entire life.'' Her voice wobbled with emotion. ''Come here, you two,'' she said, opening her arms wide.

Any doubts that Cassie might have had regarding the wisdom of her decision to accept Mac's offer were put to rest. When the hugging, kissing and crying were over, Tessie reached for Cassie's hand and asked, ''Where's the ring?''

''Actually, it's right here,'' Mac said, reaching into his shorts pocket. He pulled out a small velvet box.

This time it was Cassie whose mouth dropped open. She hadn't given a single thought to a ring. As he pulled a beautiful diamond solitaire from the box, her heart beat fiercely in her chest.

It was a simple yet elegant marquis cut that sparkled brilliantly as he held it up for her inspection. When he took her hand in his and slid the ring onto her finger, she had to bite down on her lip to keep her emotions in check.

''It fits.'' Mac sounded relieved.

''It's perfect,'' Cassie finally managed to say, gingerly moving her hand back and forth as she stared at the ring in amazement. ''Thank you.'' She reached up to give him a kiss.

Expecting to simply brush his lips, she was surprised when his mouth lingered over hers. Before either one realized it, they were both breathing heavily—much to Tessie's delight.

"Now you two wait right here. I have to get my camera and capture this moment on film," she told them before scooting out of the room.

Cassie again looked down at the ring. "I didn't know…"

He placed a finger on her lips. "Be careful."

She nodded, then continued to gaze at the ring. "I've never had a diamond before."

"Then I'd say it was the right choice," he said in a very low, seductive voice.

She almost said, "You sure know the way to a woman's heart," when Tessie returned. Cassie was grateful she chose that moment to have them pose for pictures. It was a reminder to Cassie that that was all they were doing—posing.

Mac had said the reason he'd decided to enter a marriage of convenience with her was because he knew her heart belonged to someone else. If he thought that heart was in danger of becoming attached to him, it would only make their relationship very awkward. She was certain that he wouldn't welcome any change in her feelings toward him. They were business partners, not lovers.

After Tessie had taken half a dozen snapshots of the newly engaged couple, Mac finally said, "All right, Mom. Save some of the film for the party. We have a boat to get ready for the parade."

"Before you go, let me show you what else I bought." She disappeared into the kitchen briefly, only to return carrying a red T-shirt. "I bought one for each of us." She shook it open and held it up for their inspection. On the front in the upper corner in white ink were the words "McFerrin's Crew." "And..." she held up one finger and disappeared once more.

This time when she returned she carried three baseball caps. They were navy blue with a red-and-white striped bill. Like the shirt, the caps had "McFerrin's" embroidered across the front.

These will keep the sun off our faces," she said, plopping a cap on her white head. "And let everyone know that Cassie's ours," she added with a wink at Michael.

Cassie discovered she liked belonging to the McFerrins. Most of her life she'd felt like an extra, invited to events because it was common knowledge that she had little family and nowhere else to go. But it was different with the McFerrins. Ever since that first day when she'd met Tessie, the older woman had opened her heart and her home to her. She didn't care if the special treatment she received from Mac was only because of a business agreement they'd made. When she was with him she felt special, and she was determined not to let him down in their game of make-believe.

After the first of Mac's friends arrived and she'd conquered her initial anxiety, she had no trouble pretending to be his fiancée. To her surprise, it was quite liberating. For the first time since Darryl's death she didn't have to worry about getting too friendly with a guy. Because she knew that Mac wasn't going to read more into her behavior than what was really there, she felt as if she was finally able to be herself.

For four years she'd shied away from the company

of men, keeping them at a distance to make sure that she didn't deliver a message she had no intention of sending. She wanted no long-term relationships, no commitment. Knowing that Michael wanted the same thing allowed her to be herself, to have fun and not worry that at the end of the day he'd expect to go home and take her to bed.

As Cassie expected, Tessie made sure that as each of the guests arrived, she announced the engagement. By the time the last ones had plunked their lawn chairs down on the grassy plateau near the picnic tables, Cassie had been kissed, hugged and congratulated more in one afternoon than she'd been in her entire life. Mac appeared to enjoy the attention, which had her wondering if it was all an act, like his affection for her.

Cassie didn't know how Tessie managed to keep up with all of the activity. There was the boat parade in the morning, volleyball on the lawn in the early afternoon, and swimming in the hottest part of the day. In between horseshoes and softball games, the picnic buffet had a steady line of guests filling their plates with Tessie's homemade potato salad and hamburgers hot off the grill.

By sundown, Cassie was exhausted. Tessie, however, still scooted about, making sure that everyone had something to drink while they waited for the fireworks to begin.

"Mac, I'm worried about your mother. Shouldn't she sit down for a while?" Cassie asked as Tessie moved from chair to chair talking to her guests.

"I tried to get her to sit down, but she refuses. I think she's running on pure adrenaline. She's very happy tonight."

Cassie nodded. "I know."

"Thank you for everything you did today. You were great," he told her. He looked around to make sure they were alone before saying, "This is working out even better than I expected."

A chill came over her as he reminded her of the pretense they were involved in. For most of the day she'd been having so much fun, she'd been able to forget that he was only treating her with such affection because he was trying to convince everyone they were in love.

"You cold?" he asked when she shivered.

She shook her head. "No, I'm fine. Just a little tired."

"I'll get a blanket and we'll go down to the beach. We'll get a better view of the fireworks from there," he said, then disappeared inside the house.

Beach. Blanket. Cassie wasn't sure it was the smartest idea, not in her frame of mind. Yet she didn't have much choice because, as soon as Mac returned, Tessie came over and said, "Oh, good. You're taking Cassie down to the beach to watch the fireworks."

Cassie smiled weakly. "Mac, maybe we should stay up here with the rest of the guests."

"Nonsense!" Tessie exclaimed. "You two go on down and leave us old folks up here." She shooed them away with her hands.

"I knew it was what she wanted," Mac said close to her ear as they walked toward the sandy beach. "Besides, I thought you could use a break. We'll be alone and far enough away that we won't have to pretend to be the happily engaged couple."

To Cassie it sounded as if he were tired of putting on a false show for the guests. But they were forced to continue their charade. Before they'd even spread the blanket, several of Mac's friends joined them, including Ben Herris, a man who'd known Mac since he was in grade school.

While Mac returned to the house to get more beverages, Ben took advantage of the opportunity to tell Cassie how happy he was that Mac had finally found a woman who didn't bore him after three dates.

"I think his attention span is a bit longer than three dates, don't you?" Cassie quipped.

"You know what I mean," he said with a rather sheepish grin. "If I know Mac—and I think I do—he's already told you that he hasn't exactly been looking for a wife."

"Lucky for me." She tried to make light of the comment, but it made her uncomfortable discussing the subject.

"Lucky for Mac," Ben retorted. He put his arm around her shoulder, as if revealing something very important. "The thing is this, Cassie. Mac's always been the kind of guy whose purpose in dating women was to get whatever attraction he felt for them out of his system. With you that didn't happen, because you're special, and I for one am glad it didn't, because you seem to be perfect for him."

His words did little to comfort her. Nor did the comments of the rest of his bachelor friends that day. They only confirmed what she'd originally suspected—that he'd been a player, the kind of guy who loved the chase but was soon bored with the victory. They were probably words she needed to hear, because it had been tempting to forget the real reason she was even at the McFerrins' Fourth of July.

It was after midnight by the time the party finally

came to an end, and even later by the time Mac and Cassie had put away the lawn chairs and made sure all the torches had been extinguished.

Like the ride to the lake that morning, their journey home was accomplished in silence. Strangely, Cassie felt like one of those firecrackers that had been lit earlier in the evening—as if all of her glory had come and gone and now all that was left was a fizzling trail of smoke that would soon be forgotten.

Not that she wanted Mac to say anything. She just wished they didn't have to revert to an employer-employee type of relationship. For that's how it felt to her—as if he'd hired her to do a job and while she was at work, he treated her as a valuable employee. But after hours, he wanted nothing to do with her.

As he pulled up in front of her apartment building she was tired and, consequently, rather emotional. Instead of a simple good-night, she said, "I'm glad that's done."

She knew he'd mistaken her meaning when he said irritably, "I'm sorry it was so difficult for you."

"I didn't say that I didn't have a good time. It's just that it was a lot of stress worrying about everything, that's all," she tried to explain, but from the set of his mouth she could see it wasn't doing any good.

"Well, it's over, so you can stop worrying."

He sounded impatient and she wished she hadn't said anything at all. As she gathered up her things, he came around to open her door. Then he walked her up the steps and into the building.

"Thanks. I'll be fine now," she told him when she'd unlocked the entry.

He nodded. "I'll call you later this week," he said, then walked back to the Explorer.

Cassie tried not to feel disappointed. She should have known that he wouldn't try to kiss her. Why would he? There was no one watching.

As she climbed the steps to the second floor, she mumbled to herself, "Guess it was time for the coach to turn back into a pumpkin."

ALTHOUGH CASSIE HAD CONVINCED herself that her motives for the marriage of convenience were altruistic, the longer the game of pretense went on, the more uneasy she became. Mainly she worried that somehow she'd slip up and Tessie would discover the truth. With each passing day it became more difficult to think of her arrangement with Mac as anything but deceptive. That's why after her next session at the lake, when Tessie talked nonstop wedding plans, Cassie decided it would be better if she worked alone in her studio. She'd done the preliminary sketches and could always schedule a session at the house if she thought it was necessary.

Although Tessie was disappointed, Mac seemed relieved when she told him. "That's probably a good idea."

"Then you don't mind? I thought maybe you wanted me at the lake."

"After we're married, maybe, but for right now it might be easier if you're not there every day. I told you we had the wedding plans under control, but if she has the opportunity, she'll probably get involved just like any typical mother would."

"About the wedding..." she began, wondering

how she could express her concerns without making it sound as if she wanted to end their agreement.

"I've taken care of it," he stated simply.

"You've taken care of everything?"

"Yes. We agreed I'd take charge of all the business decisions in this arrangement."

Which meant he viewed planning a wedding as a business decision. And it should have been to her, too, but as hard as she tried, she couldn't separate her emotions from her intellect on this issue.

"I didn't know that included the wedding ceremony." She tried to keep her voice even, but failed.

"You're upset."

Yes, she was, but she was afraid that if she admitted that to him, he'd see that she was getting emotionally involved—something she'd vowed not to do. "I'm just concerned that it might look odd to your mother if I'm not taking charge of some of the arrangements," she said.

"She thinks you are."

More pretense. Cassie was beginning to hate all the lies. Not for the first time did she question what kind of a mess she had gotten herself into.

"I thought you would appreciate me taking charge," he stated smoothly. "This way you won't have to suffer the same kind of anxiety the engagement created."

So he'd done it for her. "I thought I proved to you I could control my emotions that day."

"You did. Do you want to have a say in the wedding? If so, you'd better tell me now," he warned.

Suddenly Cassie felt as if she were sounding like an emotional bride-to-be. This wasn't even a real marriage. What did it matter what the wedding was like?

"No, it's all right. I'm sure you'll make it a very nice event," she stated in resignation.

"What does your calendar look like for the last weekend in July?" he asked very businesslike.

She gasped. "That's less than three weeks away!"

"Is there any reason to wait? This is a business arrangement," he reminded her.

So what did it matter when they tied the knot? she asked herself the rhetorical questions. "If it works for you, it's all right for me."

"It's one of the few weekends when I'm not on call this summer."

"It still doesn't give me much time."

"All you have to do is show up. You will show up, won't you?"

This time her gasp was one of indignation. "Of course. I couldn't hurt Tessie that way."

"I'm glad to hear that."

"Is this going to be a private ceremony?" she asked, trying to make her voice as unemotional as his as they discussed the wedding.

"I'd hoped it would be, but I'm not sure how we can ask Mom not to invite the Mums, do you?"

"No."

They went on to discuss other details of the wedding and Cassie thought she could have been a wedding planner arranging someone else's big event, so impersonal was the conversation.

Finally he ended the conversation by saying, "You're probably going to have to get together with her on the guest list."

"I'll call her today," she told him.

She had barely hung up the phone when Tessie paid her a visit. The first thought that raced through

Cassie's mind when she saw her standing on her doorstep was that Mac didn't want his mother to be driving in the city. Not that she could blame him. She'd ridden to the market with Tessie and knew that although she had the energy of a much younger person, when it came to driving, she didn't have the best reflexes.

"Forgive me for not calling, dear, but I was worried you'd be hard at work and knowing how conscientious you are, I knew if I called you'd tell me you couldn't take a break. So I thought I'd just pop in and hope that you're much too polite to send me back home without sharing some of this wonderful bundt cake I made especially for you." In a whisper, she added, "It's called peanut butter chocolate delight."

Cassie sighed. "You're right. I should be working but you know me very well, Tessie. I am not about to turn down chocolate anything." She reached out and pulled the pint-sized old lady into her apartment. Tessie wore a floral summer dress and a big, wide-brimmed straw hat that she plunked onto the antique hat tree as she passed.

"Oh, what a lovely apartment," she cooed as she stepped into the living room. "It is so you," she said, doing a three-hundred-sixty-degree turn.

Cassie took the cake from her hands. "Let me put this in the kitchen and put the kettle on, then I'll be back and we'll chat."

"Of course, dear. Would you mind if I looked around a bit?"

"No, not at all," she said, then carried the cake into the kitchen. When the water was in the kettle and on the stove, she returned to find Tessie admiring a wooden music box with a hand-carved lid. When she opened it, "The Skater's Waltz" played.

Tessie's hand moved through the air as she hummed the melody. "This is one of my favorites. I can just see the skaters gliding across ice when I listen to it. Can't you? Was this a gift from someone?"

Cassie shook her head. "It was my mother's. It's the only thing of hers that I have." To her dismay, her voice choked with emotion when she answered.

Noticing, Tessie closed the box. "You never mention her, Cassie. I don't want to pry, but I'd like to know about her."

Cassie shrugged. "There's not much to tell. She died in a fire when I was only three."

"Oh no," Tessie gushed in sympathy, taking Cassie's hands in hers. "I am so sorry. No child should have to suffer such a loss."

Normally Cassie didn't share the few memories she had of her mother, but the understanding in Tessie's face had her sitting down and pouring out feelings she hadn't acknowledged in years. Other than her aunt Ruthie, there had been few people who understood her sorrow, and the warmth in Tessie's eyes unleashed memories even Cassie had forgotten.

When she finally reached the part of the story that was the most difficult to tell, she took a deep breath, then said, "My mother would get migraine headaches so bad that she'd have to go to bed. She had one the night of the fire. That's why I was at my aunt Ruthie's. She'd taken me home with her so that my mom could go to bed. I didn't want to go so my mother told me I could take the music box with me."

"And your father?" Tessie asked gently.

"He was out of town on business and didn't find

out about it until after the house had pretty much burned to the ground. Everyone said it had started because she'd been smoking in bed.''

"How tragic. I'm so sorry," Tessie said again, covering her hand with hers. "And after it was all over?"

"My aunt Ruthie took me in. My father was gone so much of the time…" She trailed off, not wanting to say that he'd had to leave South Dakota because the memories were too painful to stay. "He sent money home for me every month, though," she added, wondering why after twenty-seven years she still felt a need to defend him.

"I'm sure he did the best he could," Tessie told her. "Most parents do. I know that's not always easy for a child to believe. Michael certainly had enough trouble believing it at times," she confessed on a sigh. "You two have so much in common. No wonder you've become so close."

Cassie didn't quite understand what she meant, but before she could ask, the teakettle whistled.

Tessie's eyes brightened. "Time for cake."

Cassie intended to continue their conversation over tea, but the older woman had come with a purpose. To settle the guest list for the wedding.

"You'll want your aunt there, won't you, dear?" she said, pulling a tablet from her purse. As she dug for a pen, she pulled out an envelope from the photo shop. "Oh look. I almost forgot to give you the pictures."

They were snapshots from the Fourth of July, the ones Tessie had taken right after she and Mac had told her they were engaged. Cassie studied each one, amazed at how normal they looked. They could have been any couple in love.

Tessie showed her which ones were her favorites and Cassie pretended to be the glowing bride-to-be, as talk of pictures became the wedding guest list discussion. While they ate the peanut butter cake iced with chocolate, they drafted a list of names. Most of the guests were Tessie's friends—which suited Cassie just fine. It was more her day than Cassie's.

When the last of the tea had been sipped, Tessie announced it was time for her to head back to the lake if she didn't want to get stuck in the rush-hour traffic. That thought had Cassie packing up her bundt cake container and urging her toward the door.

"I'm sorry to have interrupted your work, dear," Tessie said as she reached for her hat. Without looking in the mirror, she plopped it on her white head and said, "Do you forgive me?"

"There's nothing to forgive," she said, giving her a hug.

"I think it's been good to have this girl talk, don't you?"

"Yes, I do."

"And now we have the guest list," she said, patting the pocket where she'd slipped the piece of paper. "I know Michael said the two of you wanted to take care of all the arrangements, but I insisted I at least help out with the invitations."

"That is very kind of you, and I appreciate it," Cassie said sincerely.

"With so little time to prepare, you need an extra pair of hands."

Feeling a bit guilty, Cassie asked, "I hope you don't think we're rushing things?"

"Good heavens no, girl. I saw this day coming the first time Michael brought you to my house. I could see by the way he looked at you that he'd fallen in love.'' She snapped her fingers, and added, ''Just like that.''

Again guilt washed over Cassie. It was obvious that Tessie saw only what she wanted to see.

''And who am I to question love at first sight? You know what happened between me and my Frank,'' she said on a romantic sigh as she turned to open the door. She waved goodbye and was a couple of steps into the hallway when she stopped. ''Oh. I almost forgot. The Mums are meeting at my house for tea a week from Sunday to discuss ideas for our Christmas show. Would you be able to help us out with the stage props?''

Cassie didn't hesitate to agree. ''I'll bring my sketch pad. Just tell me the time.''

As soon as she was alone, she went back to the kitchen to get the photographs Tessie had left. As she looked at each one again, she realized they were the only photos of Mac she had. He was such a handsome man…and he'd make such a great subject….

She went into her studio.

CASSIE WONDERED how many brides received their wedding plans in the mail. True to his word, Mac made all the arrangements, then sent her a detailed list that included a schedule for the day of the wedding. According to the plan, all she had to do was find a dress, ask someone to be her maid of honor and pray that her nerves would withstand the pressure of the next few weeks.

She turned to Claudia for help with all three. Expecting another lecture as to the wisdom of her marriage, Cassie was surprised when Claudia eagerly accepted the honor of being her bridesmaid. She was grateful to have the support of her best friend as they shopped for a wedding dress that would be elegant yet simple enough for an outdoor wedding.

Thanks to Claudia's sister, who owned a dress boutique, she found exactly what she was looking for, a lovely creation Claudia described as the bridal gown to stop boat traffic. A body-skimming sheath made of ivory lace, it hugged her slender figure, accentuating curves normally hidden by her loose-fitting skirts and tops. Instead of a veil, she'd wear a garland of flowers in her hair.

The next stop on their agenda was the day spa, where once again Claudia had a connection. They both made appointments for a massage and facial the morning of the wedding, to be followed by hair styling and makeup.

Before heading for home, Claudia suggested they visit a jeweler. When Cassie gave her a questioning look, she said, "A gift for the groom, maybe?"

Cassie was grateful for the reminder, for she didn't want to give Tessie any reason to think this was anything but a normal wedding. So with Claudia's help she picked out a pair of gold cuff links to be given to Mac on their wedding day, determined not to give anyone a single reason to suspect they were marrying for anything but love.

For Cassie, it was a whirlwind three weeks. Although she'd been married, she'd never been a bride in the true sense of the word. She and Darryl had run off to a justice of the peace to say their vows. With two strangers as witnesses, they'd spent all of five minutes pledging a lifetime of promises that had never been kept.

She wasn't sure that having all the fancy trimmings was going to make this marriage any different. What she did know was that she was entering into this union with her eyes wide-open. She had no illusions of happily ever after, no unrealistic expectations that Mac would love her and only her.

Other people did have those expectations, however, which she was reminded of when she went to Tessie's for tea the following Sunday. When she walked into the McFerrin living room, she was greeted with a chorus of "Surprise."

What Tessie had told her was to be a planning session for the Mums Christmas program was actually a wedding shower. An arch of white balloons marked the spot where she, the guest of honor, was to sit. Stacked high beside the chair was a pile of packages all wrapped in silver and white.

For Cassie, who'd never had a shower of any kind before, it was impossible not to be touched and she felt her throat clog with emotion as she attempted to tell them how much she appreciated their gesture of kindness. Besides the Mums, the group included Claudia plus several of the staff from the vet clinic.

They played the dice game, unscrambled wedding words and made a wedding dress for Cassie out of toilet paper. Every guest gave the bride a piece of wedding advice, then Cassie opened each of the prettily wrapped packages, blushing at the contents of several of them. Lingerie designed for the new bride brought oohs and aahs from the guests, as well as knowing snickers of amusement.

Getting gifts from well-wishing friends was one aspect of the arrangement she hadn't considered. Monogrammed towels with the letter *M* boldly stitched across the bottom made her feel like a fraud, especially since she'd already decided she'd keep her surname. Crystal vases and sterling silver serving pieces seemed less personal, yet were a reminder that no one except Claudia knew the true reason for her marriage. Yet even her best friend had given her a photo album engraved with their name and wedding date.

With as much grace as she could muster, Cassie thanked everyone for their thoughtfulness, then watched as Claudia made a bridal bouquet from the bows off the packages. When Tessie announced it was time to eat, Cassie had little appetite, but once again put on a smile and pretended to be happy as guests dined on cucumber sandwiches and drank a concoction of fruit juice and champagne Tessie called her Summer Sizzlers.

For Cassie it was an afternoon she would remember for a long time to come. She thought about how different it would be if only she and Mac were marrying because they were in love.

As Tessie announced the final prize to be given away, Agnes passed around paper and pencils one more time. "On this piece of paper you are to write the honeymoon destination of Michael and Cassie."

Honeymoon? Michael had said nothing about a honeymoon.

"The guest who guesses the correct destination— or the one geographically closest to the correct destination, will go home with this lovely fuschia," Tessie said, holding up the flowering plant in a hanging basket.

Heads bent and pencils moved across the papers. After several minutes, Tessie declared, "Time's up.

Cassie will now tell us where the honeymoon will be.''

All eyes turned to Cassie, who could feel the blood drain from her face. Then Tessie giggled and said, ''Just kidding. The bride doesn't know where she's going. Michael's been a good groom and kept it a secret. I, however, know, and will be the judge of our final contest. Agnes, collect the answers, and I'll read them in the kitchen.''

Agnes went around collecting the slips of paper, then gave Cassie a mischievous smile as she handed them over to Tessie, who disappeared into the kitchen. Within only a few minutes, she was back. She handed the plant to Betty Jean, who gasped in delight.

''It was a guess! I had no idea it would be right!'' she crooned.

''Now, remember. Don't breathe a word to the bride,'' Tessie warned with a finger to her lips.

All the guests laughed and resumed their party chatter. Cassie, however, could think of one thing and one thing only. The honeymoon.

Did Mac really expect her to go away with him following the wedding?

Chapter Eleven

Mac spent most of Sunday nursing a hangover. Not since his college days had he suffered what his mother had always referred to as "bottle flu" and he'd forgotten just how nasty a guy could feel the morning after.

On this particular morning after, he was wishing he'd said no when his buddies had asked if they could throw him a bachelor party. He knew it was a rite of passage. Before the wedding day, a night with the guys had to be set aside to make sure that the groom would know just what he was missing.

With the way his head was pounding, Mac didn't think he'd be missing much. The women he'd seen last night had all looked the same, the cigars had all tasted stale after a few puffs and the liquor had gone down easy but left lasting effects he hoped he would never experience again.

What had started out as a small group of friends having a few drinks at the bar had ended up as a party of over twenty people—most of them strangers to Mac. When word had spread through the crowd that he was a man about to lose his freedom, there wasn't a guy in the bar who hadn't bought him a drink.

Mac squinted at the memory. He'd played some pool, thrown a few darts and drunk far too many of the shots that kept coming his way. At some point food had been delivered to the table. And there had been the singing telegram—an off-duty "police-woman" named Bambi who'd arrived in her uniform and left wearing nothing but a couple of badges and a G-string. Then, the party had moved to someone's house, and in the wee hours of the morning, the best man had finally dragged him home.

As he searched his medicine cabinet for something that would give him relief, there was only one thought going through Mac's head. Thank goodness he'd done this one week instead of one night before the wedding. He plopped a couple of tablets in a glass of water, swallowed it with a grimace, then stumbled back into bed where he stayed most of the day.

To his relief, there were no emergencies at the clinic that interrupted his healing process. It wasn't until late afternoon that the phone rang. It was his mother calling to say that Cassie was about to leave and head back to her apartment with a vanload of gifts. *Their* gifts. And wouldn't it be nice if he were to be there waiting for her so that the poor girl wouldn't have to carry everything in by herself?

In his present condition, he hardly felt like going anywhere. The tablets had settled his stomach and his head no longer felt as if an army of soldiers were marching across it, but he still felt like yesterday's garbage. With a groan he pulled on a pair of jeans and a T-shirt, slipped on a pair of deck shoes and headed for his Explorer.

As soon as he arrived at Cassie's, he was sorry he'd

made the effort. She did not look happy to see him. Actually, she looked a bit irritated with him.

"Look at all this!" she said in disgust as she bent over the open cargo area. "See what happens when you deceive people?"

He was tempted to turn around, get back in his Explorer and go home. But he'd already done the hard part—gotten out of bed. "Do you want my help or not?"

"Not." She lifted a stack of boxes in her arms and started toward the entrance.

"Okay, fine." He started to walk back to his car but then stopped. She hadn't even told him what was bugging her. He caught up with her, took the boxes from her hands and ordered, "Get the door for me."

She didn't argue with him, but followed his instructions. Without another word they worked together until all of the packages sat on her living room floor.

"Thank you," she said, as he stood with his hands on his hips facing her.

It sounded like a reluctant thank-you, which had him doing a slow burn. What the hell was her problem? Determined to find out, he said, "You always this ugly when someone gives you gifts?"

That had her eyes flashing. "Maybe you should have been the one to sit through three hours of people showering you with presents and talking nonstop about a wedding they think is the most romantic event of the century."

He raked a hand across the back of his head. "That's what this is all about?"

"Do you know what the door prize at the shower was?" she demanded as she paced the floor.

He stared at her in disbelief. How the hell was he

supposed to know the answer to something like that and why would he even care?

She didn't wait for him to respond. "It was a fuschia. And you know how they determined who would get the fuschia?"

Again she didn't wait for him to reply. "They played a game. Guess the honeymoon." She looked at him as if that should have some great meaning to him.

"And your point is?" he asked.

Which had her rolling her eyes and slapping her palms against her thighs. "You never mentioned a honeymoon as being a part of this deal."

"I just assumed you knew it would be. If you have a wedding, you have a honeymoon."

"Your mother said you're taking me some place romantic," she said with disdain.

"What else would you expect me to say to her? That we were going back to our separate apartments and not speaking to each other except when duty required we pay her a visit?" This time his was the voice with the causticity.

"There was no mention of honeymoon on the wedding schedule you gave me." Degas, as if suddenly aware of disharmony in the living room, came sauntering out of Cassie's office with a meow. To Mac's surprise, he didn't rub up against Cassie's legs, but came and sat at his feet.

"Degas, mind your manners," Cassie shrieked at him in pretty much the same tone as she'd been using on Mac. The cat didn't like it. He curled himself around Mac's legs.

"He senses that you're upset," Mac said in a calm voice, bending to scratch the cat behind the ears.

"Of course I'm upset. I get all these presents I don't deserve—" her arms flapped aimlessly in the direction of the boxes "—and I discover I'm supposed to go off to some romantic place with my pretend husband...why didn't you have honeymoon on the schedule?"

"Because when I sent that schedule to you I hadn't yet made the arrangements. It was only when my mother asked about it that I decided it would be a good idea to make plans. I figured we could always say one of us became ill and postpone."

"So you never intended that there would be a honeymoon?"

He realized that he'd be lying if he said he didn't. When he'd made the reservations to spend four days at a bed-and-breakfast on Lake Superior's North Shore, he'd thought it would be a good way for the two of them to adjust to married life—or at least married life as they would know it.

He avoided answering her question by saying, "If you don't want to go away for a few days, just say so. As I said, we can always tell everyone that we had to postpone the honeymoon because one of us got sick."

"More lying," she said quietly, then sank down onto the sofa. "This is only going to get more complicated, isn't it."

"We're pretending to be married. How much more complicated can it get?"

"We shouldn't be lying to your mother," she said, her voice dripping with remorse.

"What are you saying? That you want to call the whole thing off?" It was a question he hated to ask, but one for which he needed an answer.

"I don't know. I'm going to have to think about it."

"Cassie, the wedding is six days away," he reminded her.

"I know."

Six days. If she didn't change her mind they'd be Mr. and Mrs. McFerrin. He'd be a married man—something he had sworn would never happen. So now that there was a possibility it might not happen, why was he feeling threatened?

"Look, I'm going to leave and let you think things over," he told her. "You can let me know your decision."

She simply nodded.

As he left her apartment building, he realized that he'd just made a startling discovery. He couldn't let the choice be hers. One way or another, he was going to have to find a way to make Cassie his wife.

"HAPPY IS THE BRIDE the sun shines on," Tessie greeted Cassie with a hug when she and Claudia arrived on the day of her wedding. "Oh, your hair. It's lovely! You're going to make a beautiful bride. I've seen Michael in his tuxedo. He looks so handsome!"

Cassie could imagine. Mac looked good in everything.

"Now do you have something old, something new, something borrowed, something blue?" Tessie asked.

Cassie looked down at her hands. "Oh my gosh. I left my grandmother's ring at home."

"The old," Claudia explained.

"Don't worry. I have something I've saved to give to you today." Tessie reached into her pocket and pulled out a small box wrapped with a silver bow and gave it to Cassie.

When she opened the tiny package, she found a small silver ring with a pearl set in a flower-shaped setting. "It's lovely," she said, lifting the ring from the satin lining.

"It belonged to Patricia Collier. She gave it to me when she was sent away and asked me to keep it for Michael. He never wanted it, which I always thought was quite sad. Told me I should keep it. So I did and now I want you to have it," Tessie said quietly.

Patricia Collier? Cassie had never heard the name before, although it was obvious from Tessie's explanation that Mac's mother thought she should know who the other woman was. Not wanting to raise Tessie's suspicions regarding her relationship with Mac, she simply said, "Thank you. I will treasure it."

"I put a silver chain in the box. If the ring doesn't fit your finger you can slip it on the chain and wear it around your neck—under that beautiful dress, of course. It'll be your something old for the wedding." Tessie slipped her arm through Cassie's. "Now come see what they've done with the gazebo."

They were the Mums, Cassie's unofficial wedding coordinators. Mac had told her they'd insisted on decorating the yard for the wedding and that he hadn't had the heart to say no.

That's why Cassie shouldn't have been surprised to see the abundance of flowers. They were everywhere on the gazebo. Still, she gasped at the beautiful scene before her.

"It's like something you'd see in a movie," she said on a note of wonder as she climbed the steps of the gazebo and stood among the most exotic colored blooms she had ever seen.

"You've done so much for the Mums, dear, they were thrilled to be able to do something for you," Tessie told her.

"Everyone's been so nice. I...I don't deserve this," she said, unable to keep the emotion from her voice.

Again Tessie hugged her. "Nonsense. You are every bit as beautiful as those flowers and I am so happy you will be standing here with my son saying those vows. Now, let's put away such foolish thoughts and go inside. Claudia and I have to get you put away before Michael arrives."

"Are you going to be okay?" Claudia asked a few minutes later when they were alone in the guest bedroom.

She nodded. "Yes. I'm just a little emotional, which is to be expected, right?"

"It's not too late to back out, Cass," Claudia said with concern in her eyes.

But Cassie knew she wouldn't. She'd made her decision shortly after Michael had left on Sunday evening. As she'd fussed over where to put all the lovely gifts she'd received at the shower, she'd realized that it wasn't guilt that was causing her so much anxiety. It was her feelings for Michael.

But it wasn't until Tessie's visit the following morning that she realized why. Mac's mother had come on the pretext of needing answers to a couple of last-minute details Michael had assigned to her regarding the wedding. Cassie knew it was more likely that Mac had sent his mother as a reminder of just why they had planned to be married in the first place.

Tessie had told Cassie that it was natural for a bride to have pre-wedding jitters. It had happened to her. As much as she loved Frank, the night before they were to say their vows, she suffered a moment of panic and nearly called off the wedding.

Then she'd taken Cassie's hands in hers and looked her straight in the eye and said, "Sometimes love happens so suddenly we can't believe it's there. It's a little scary, but once you trust your heart, you won't regret it."

At that moment Cassie knew that she'd been frightened of her feelings for Mac ever since the night she'd met him at Dinner Date. It wasn't the thought of having to pretend to be in love that was causing so much anxiety in her life; it was the thought of having to pretend to *not* be in love with him.

"You're a wise woman, Tessie, and I am so lucky to be getting you for a mother-in-law," Cassie had told her.

Tessie had hugged her and said, "Michael's the one who's lucky."

"Cassie, did you hear me?" Claudia interrupted her musings. "It's not too late to change your mind."

"Yes, it is, Claudia," Cassie told her. "I've fallen in love with Mac."

Claudia's mouth dropped open. "I don't know if I should hug you or scold you."

"I think I could use a hug more than a scolding," she answered, spreading her arms.

"And does the groom know how the bride feels?" Claudia asked.

"No, and he's not going to find out. This is a business arrangement. Nothing more, nothing less," she said as she unzipped the plastic garment bag covering her wedding dress.

"But how are you going to live with the man and not tell him how you feel?"

Cassie held up her hand. "You forget. I've had a lot of experience. Now let's stop talking and get down to business. We have a wedding to attend."

WEDDINGS ALWAYS MADE CASSIE CRY. It had been that way ever since she was a little girl. So why she thought her own would be any different was a mystery to her. Maybe because when she and Darryl had been married by a justice of the peace, she hadn't shed a single tear.

But then there hadn't been a brass quartet playing the "Trumpet Voluntary" by Purcell, either. Nor was she wearing a beautiful wedding gown of Victorian lace that had everyone sighing as she made her entrance on the arm of Emmet Sandberg.

She felt like a superstar model as she climbed the steps to the gazebo amid a shower of rose petals. Except this superstar model couldn't keep the tears from pooling in her eyes. Mac saw them when he took her hand and placed it in the crook of his arm.

Any hope she had that once the music stopped, the tears would, too, disappeared when the minister began the ceremony. Moisture that had only glazed her eyes on her entrance began to spill over onto her cheeks. With an extreme effort she managed not to sob, but she couldn't prevent the trembling in her shoulders.

At one point in the ceremony, Mac pulled the silk handkerchief from his pocket and dabbed at her cheeks, which produced a few sighs from the guests. Anyone who hadn't realized she was crying, at that point, was left in little doubt. When she said her vows, her voice broke and she even hiccuped, much to her horror. When the actually ceremony was finally over and the minister announced that they were now husband and wife, she breathed a sigh of relief.

Michael kissed her tenderly on the lips, then whispered in her ear, "At least pretend to be happy." To the guests seated on the white folding chairs, it looked as if he were whispering sweet nothings in her ear. Only Cassie knew how far that was from the truth.

"They're tears of joy," she whispered back, and told each of the guests the same thing as she received hugs, kisses and warm wishes in the reception line. Everyone nodded in understanding, a few adding what they thought were funny comments. Such things like, "I'd be crying, too, if I were facing a life with this guy."

Mac smiled and good-naturedly accepted the teasing, but Cassie knew that she needed to make him forget that she'd cried at all. So for the rest of the afternoon she smiled and laughed and treated him as if he were the most important man in the universe. By the time they were ready to make their departure, the guests had no reason to suspect she wasn't happy.

And she *was* happy. It took no acting on her part to be the radiant bride. Although Mac appeared to be rather tense at times throughout the day, she enjoyed every minute of their wedding reception. When it came time for her to throw her bouquet of coral roses and leave in the big white limousine parked in Tessie's driveway, she was feeling confident that she'd made the right decision in going through with the marriage.

She wasn't convinced, however, that Mac shared

her sentiment. As soon as they were seated in the luxurious car, he loosened the bow tie around his neck and poured himself a glass of Scotch from the portable bar.

"Thank God that's over," he said, then downed the Scotch in one gulp.

"I thought it was nice."

He set the glass down with a thud and leaned back against the cushioned seat. "Guess we have different definitions of nice."

She paused, unsure what she should say next. His body language wasn't exactly inviting conversation. "Your mother looked happy."

"Yes, she did," he agreed.

Judging by the look on his face, she wasn't sure if he thought even that was important enough to balance his dislike of the afternoon. "It is the reason for the whole charade," she reminded him, annoyed by his attitude.

That caused his face to harden. "You played your part well." There was no admiration in the words.

"Just doing my job," she said with equal disdain.

Silence stretched between them, and Cassie wondered if it was even worth the effort to try to make conversation when he was obviously in a foul mood. When he turned on the small overhead TV suspended from the roof and tuned in the Twins baseball game, she reached for her purse and pulled out a novel she'd brought along to the beauty salon that morning.

She wondered what the limousine driver must be thinking. They didn't exactly look like newlyweds, sitting on opposite ends of the plush interior, Mac watching baseball and his bride reading a true crime novel.

Although she could hardly call what she was doing reading. Her eyes may have been looking at the printed words on the pages, but her thoughts were on the night ahead of her. What kind of a wedding night would it be if the bride and groom weren't even speaking to each other?

According to the revised wedding day schedule that Mac had given her earlier in the week, they were on their way to his condominium, where they would change their clothes and then set out for their honeymoon. Cassie's suitcases were already at his place, as were several pieces of furniture from her apartment, including her bed. Knowing that Tessie expected them to live together, Cassie had agreed with Mac that the more things of Cassie's Tessie found at his place, the better it would look.

Seeing how Mac was behaving in the limousine, Cassie was relieved, however, that she hadn't given up her apartment. Even though her bed now occupied the guest bedroom in Mac's place, she could still sleep on the divan in her studio if she found the need for her own space.

Tonight could be one of those times, she thought as Mac unlocked the door to his condominium. Cassie thought she might as well say something right now rather than let the awkwardness continue.

"If you'll give me a ride back to my apartment, we can make it a better night for both of us," she said as she stepped inside. She saw her suitcase sitting close by and automatically reached for it.

"You agreed to do the honeymoon," he reminded her. "Right after you told me you wanted to go through the wedding."

"You sent your mother over, didn't you? You

knew that if I saw how much our marriage meant to her, I wouldn't be able to back out," she said accusingly.

He smiled for the first time since they'd left the lake. "It worked, didn't it?"

Once again that grin did things to her insides. She smiled provocatively and said, "I'm here, aren't I?"

"But you want to leave."

"You don't really want to spend four days with me and nothing but the north woods for company, do you?"

"I'm not the one who's asking to be taken back to my apartment." The smile was gone, replaced with a guarded expression, but it was his eyes she responded to, and the challenge she saw in them.

She decided to be bold. "I enjoy your company, Mac. I think we could have a good time at the North Shore."

"And is that why you asked me to take you home?"

"No, I told you I was willing to go on a honeymoon, but how do you expect me to behave when, ever since we've left your mother's place, you've been treating me as if I'm an unwanted relative who's come to camp on your doorstep?"

"I don't think of you that way. I enjoy your company, too, Cassie."

It was the nicest thing he'd said to her all day. And even better, there was no one watching. "Then wouldn't it be silly *not* to go to the North Shore?"

He didn't disagree.

THE MINUTE CASSIE SAW the view out of the windows of their room at the bed-and-breakfast inn, she knew why Mac called the North Shore one of his very favorite places to be. It was like being at the ocean, so vast was the expanse of Lake Superior visible to their eyes. She went to bed at night hearing the slap of the waves against the shore, and woke up each morning to the glorious splendor of the sun rising over the water.

Situated in a wooded grove, the inn offered solitude and privacy with its own pebble beach on the lake and a sauna out back. Although recently constructed, it had the smell of old pine, with a large cobblestone fireplace in the dining room that was often lit on the cool summer evenings.

Since it was Cassie's first trip to the recreational area, she allowed Mac to be her tour guide, taking his suggestions as they mapped a different route for each of the days they were to be in the region. Like any first-time visitor, Cassie wanted to cram as much activity into their days as possible, overwhelmed by the number of waterfalls and state parks just waiting to be explored.

As they traveled the shoreline between Duluth and Grand Portage, Cassie realized that Mac had chosen their particular bed-and-breakfast because it was located close to Grand Marais, a scenic harbor community with a business district dotted with antique shops and art galleries. Even the room they stayed in was known as Artist's Point, after the rock jetty that stretched out into a bay area and provided inspiration for so many artists.

With the passing of each day, Cassie fell more in love with Mac, although she was careful not to let him see her true feelings. It was a vacation filled with many firsts for her. Never had she fished in a stream for trout. Nor had she hiked through woods populated with white-tailed deer and timber wolves. And never had she slept in the same room with a man and been so tempted yet not made love to him.

On the four-hour drive to the inn, she'd worried that sharing a room with Mac would be awkward. Yet after the initial "I'll take this bed and you take that one," there had been no reason for her to think there would be any problems.

Until the final day of their stay. After overexerting herself when they'd rented bicycles earlier in the day, Cassie told Mac that she was going to let him explore Pincushion Mountain on his own that afternoon. While he was gone, she walked to the small town of Grand Marais, stopped in a few shops, then realized that what she really needed was to soak her aching muscles in a whirlpool bath.

Mac had told her he wouldn't be back before six and it was only four-thirty. After a long, leisurely soak, she climbed out, towel-dried and slipped on her bra and underpants. Next she dried her hair, then slipped the silver chain with the ring Tessie'd given her back around her neck. She'd fallen into the habit of wearing it beneath her clothes, liking the idea of having something special next to her heart.

Having left her clean clothes in the bedroom, she padded out across the thick carpet and pulled open the drawer on the pine chest at the same time that Mac opened the door.

"Oh! I didn't expect you'd be back yet," she said, embarrassed yet aware that the pink bikini she'd worn swimming revealed just as much as her underwear.

But she was not in a bathing suit, as Mac's face

told her. His eyes roved up and down her figure, and then up and down it again.

"Why are you back early?" she asked, trying to defuse the tension that was suddenly so great she thought he might trip over it if he walked toward her.

He didn't walk toward her. Not that it mattered. The way those eyes were looking at her he might as well have been touching her.

Then she said, "I *am* your wife, Mac."

It was all the invitation he needed. He was at her side in a flash, scooping her into his arms and kissing her with a passion so strong Cassie had to cling to his shoulders. When he finally lifted his mouth from hers, she was breathing heavily, but he didn't let her go. His lips blazed a trail of kisses across her neck, down her shoulders, to the soft flesh spilling over the cups of her bra.

Cassie moaned in delight at the exquisite pleasure his touch produced. Then just as quickly as it had started, it was over.

"Where did you get that?" he asked, pointing to the pearl ring dangling on the chain around Cassie's neck.

"Your mother gave it to me. She said it belonged to someone named Patricia Collier. She acted as if I should know she was."

"I guess she figured that if I had asked you to marry you, I'd told you that Tessie's not my birth mother," he answered. "She adopted me when I was four."

"I didn't know. I'm sorry."

He shrugged. "It's nothing to be sorry about. Tessie's a wonderful mother, the only one I remember."

"That's not why I said I was sorry. When Tessie

gave me the ring, she said it was supposed to be for you, but that you didn't want it. I didn't think to ask you if you would mind if I wore it," she said honestly.

He shoved his hands into his jeans. "Of course, you can wear it. The reason I didn't want it was because at the time of Patricia's death, I didn't know what I'd do with a pearl ring. And since I've never planned to get married, I figured Tessie ought to keep it. But now she's given it to you, which I suppose is what should be done with it. You *are* my wife."

"Yes, I am," she agreed with a smile, but he didn't return that smile.

"About what happened here..." He moved his finger in a circular motion in the air. "In the future, it'd be better for both of us if you didn't run around half-naked," he said, then turned around and left without another word.

Cassie felt as if she'd been slapped across the face. She'd seen desire in his eyes and tasted it in his kiss. And she'd made it clear to him that she felt the same way. Yet he'd left.

Because he didn't want a real wife. Just a pretend one.

She'd come on the honeymoon knowing she had four days to show him how much she cared about him, to prove to him that they could have fun together, to try to make him see that their marriage didn't have to be fake.

And she'd failed.

She reached for the pearl flower ring and rubbed it absently. It was a gift of love from one mother to another and now a gift to her, the woman who loved their son. Yet it was the reason she and Mac hadn't made love.

As she stared at the ring she realized that it had probably also saved her from making a big mistake. If Mac had any feelings for her at all, it was only because there wasn't anything physical between them. She'd been in danger of forgetting that he was a man who loved the chase but not the victory. Once he'd made love with her, he'd soon tire of her, just as he had all the other women in his life.

And that was something she didn't want to happen.

Chapter Twelve

Cassie was surprised at how easy it was to adjust to living with Mac. Not that they lived together in the biblical sense of the word. Sharing a home with him was easy—or at least easier than it had ever had been with Darryl.

It felt strange to not think of her ex-husband with hate. For so many years she'd woken up each morning and the first thought on her mind had been to make sure that he didn't spoil her day.

Now he was seldom in her thoughts at all. All the anger, the bitterness she'd harbored for years, had quietly gone away. She knew it was due to a combination of many things—her success as an artist, finally having the debts from his past settled, and, of course, Mac.

She hadn't expected she would ever want to share her life with another man, but then she hadn't expected she'd meet a guy like Mac and agree to a marriage of convenience, either. Logic told her she shouldn't have been happy, but she was.

She was glad she had moved some of her things to Mac's condominium before they left on the honeymoon. While they were gone, Tessie had come and put fresh flowers in the vases and dropped off Degas, whom she'd been cat-sitting, on the morning of the day they were due to arrive home.

She'd also left a stack of photographs she'd had developed. Snapshots from the wedding that Cassie had slipped into the album Claudia had given her— the one with their names and their wedding date engraved on the front.

She looked at the photos often during the following weeks. She wondered how Mac could look at them and not see what was so clearly showing on her face—her love for him. Then she wondered if maybe he had noticed and was choosing to ignore it.

It had been three weeks since their honeymoon and not once had he touched her—except for those times when they'd be at Tessie's. Then he was very affectionate.

It was slowly driving Cassie insane, being married yet not sharing all of the intimacies of married life. She'd wake up in the middle of the night and think about him in the room next door, remembering the sounds he made while he slept. Wishing she could be lying beside him, feeling his heartbeat, touching his warm body.

Frustrated, she did the only thing she knew would get her through her sleeplessness. She worked.

LIFE SETTLED INTO a normal routine—or what Mac guessed a normal routine would be if he had a normal marriage. Although Cassie had moved most of her things to his condominium, she still worked at her studio in her apartment—which was where she usually was when he came home each night.

She'd taken him literally when he'd said he didn't

care if she didn't cook for him. Not once since they'd been back from their honeymoon had she even been home for dinner, let alone made it for him.

He knew it was his own fault. If he asked her to be there, she'd be there. She did everything he asked. Only he didn't want to have to ask her to do things for him. He wanted her to do them of her own free will.

"Dr. Mac? Did you forget about the patient in room one?" Tabitha stuck her head inside his office door.

He had forgotten. He was doing it a lot lately—forgetting. He knew all of the women at the clinic thought it was because he was a newlywed. "The man's got only one thing on his mind," they'd tease. Little did they know how wrong they were. He had dozens of things on his mind—though all of them were concerning Cassie.

She was driving him crazy with her mixed messages. Her definition of being just friends was the biggest come-on he'd ever had from a woman. Was it any wonder that he couldn't stop thinking about her?

"Dr. Mac?"

"I'm coming," he said, glad to have a patient to distract him from such thoughts. But when he opened the door to room one, there sat Cassie with Degas.

"What are you doing here?" he asked, which had Tabitha looking at him rather curiously. He discreetly closed the door before saying another word.

"Degas needed his annual checkup and I figured I might as well come here," she answered. "Should I have asked for Lynn?"

"No, it's all right," he answered, trying to concentrate on the task at hand—examining the Abyssinian. But out of the corners of his eyes he could see the gentle swell of Cassie's enticing bosom as she leaned over the table, her arms resting beside Degas.

"Your mother called to remind us that she has tickets for the theater next Thursday. She asked if we could have dinner first."

"When did all this come up?" he asked irritably. "She knows Thursday's my night out with the guys."

"Don't worry about it. I'll take her."

"She won't like wasting a ticket."

"It won't go to waste. I'll find a friend to go with us," she said in her usual calm, accommodating tone.

"Fine. Take a friend," he mumbled, eager to finish the exam so she could take Degas and her lovely bosom out of the clinic.

She hadn't been gone long when his phone rang. It was his mother, calling to scold him about the theater. He should have expected as much. What he didn't expect was that he'd change his mind and say he'd forgo his night out with the guys.

But then he didn't know that Thursday was the anniversary of Cassie's first husband's death.

"WASN'T THAT THE LOVELIEST production of *Camelot* you've ever seen?" Tessie asked Michael and Cassie as they left the theater in downtown Minneapolis.

"It was rather sweet," Cassie agreed.

Michael simply grunted and said, "*Camelot* is *Camelot*."

"Pay no attention to him, Cassie. He doesn't appreciate the fine arts the way we do," Tessie said with a tug on her arm. Just as they were about to cross the street, a clap of thunder split the air.

"It sounds like rain coming," Michael said as he hurried the two women along.

They had just reached the Explorer when it began falling in torrents that made travel nearly impossible. As Michael started the engine, he turned on the radio to get a weather report, only to hear that there were several flash flood warnings for the western suburbs.

"Oh my! You don't suppose they mean Navarre, do you?" Tessie asked nervously. "How will I get home?"

As the rain continued to pelt the windshield, Michael said, "You're not going home, Mother. You'll stay in town with us."

"Don't be silly. You're newlyweds. You don't need your mother butting in on you," Tessie protested.

"Mac's right," Cassie agreed, wishing they were already back at the condominium and out of the rain. "And you could never butt in on anyone. We'd love to have you."

"You can have the spare bedroom," Mac said.

And my bed. The implication hit Cassie like one of those loud claps of thunder echoing around them. If Tessie slept in her room, that meant that she would have to sleep in Mac's room. In *his* bed. Her heart raced at the thought.

"If that's what you think is best, of course I'll listen to you," Tessie said in a tiny, tired voice.

Cassie didn't dare glance across to Michael. He had to be thinking the same thing as she. Pretending to be married while visiting Tessie at her home was one thing. Having her spending the night with them at his place was another.

Trying to act as if nothing out of the ordinary was happening, Cassie showed her mother-in-law to the guest bedroom, grateful now that she'd taken the extra time to change the sheets and put away all of her clothes that morning. When Tessie saw her makeup in the guest bathroom, she said, "I don't blame you for wanting a separate bathroom to yourself. Isn't it nice to be able to leave your things out?"

"Yes, it's certainly easier having my own space," Cassie agreed as she handed her a fresh set of towels. "That's why I use the closet in the guest bedroom for my things, too. That way I'm not crowding Mac," she added, just in case Tessie decided to hang up her dress and saw all of Cassie's things inside.

She was glad that she had when Tessie asked, "Do you have a nightgown I might use?"

Cassie opened a drawer and pulled out two nightshirts—one cotton, one satin. She handed the cotton one to Tessie.

"Thank you, dear," the older woman said gratefully. "If you don't mind, I think I'll turn in. I do believe that the theater wore me out."

Cassie suspected that what she really was trying to do was give her and Mac some time alone. Cassie said good-night, then took her satin nightshirt and left.

Mac was in the kitchen, leaning up against the counter, drinking a soda. "Is she all settled?"

Cassie nodded. "She said to say good-night."

"She went to bed already?"

"I think she wants to give us time alone," Cassie whispered.

He raked a hand across the back of his neck. "I'm

sorry, Cassie. I didn't expect anything like this would happen.'' He deliberately kept his voice low.

She shrugged. ''We'll make do. It's not like we haven't slept in the same room before, is it?''

''Why don't you go on in first? I have some work I want to do before I turn in,'' he told her.

She nodded, knowing that he was giving her the opportunity to fall asleep before he came to bed. ''Good night.''

She'd only been in Mac's bedroom once—the day he'd shown her around the condo, explaining where everything was. She knew it had a king-size bed, an entertainment system, a whole wall of books, massive dark furniture and a private bath that was considerably larger than hers.

She didn't know that his pillows would smell like his aftershave. Or that he'd have a photograph of the two of them on his nightstand. She saw it as she lay her head on the pillow. It was from their wedding day and was one she hadn't seen.

As she slipped under the covers, she tried to lie as close to the edge of the bed as possible. How long Mac waited before coming to bed, she didn't know, for the next time she woke, it was completely dark in the room. She knew he was in bed beside her, because she could hear him breathing.

She rolled over and saw that he was sprawled across the center of the bed. His arms and chest were bare. She lifted the covers and sighed. He wore pajama bottoms.

As her eyes adjusted to the lack of light, she was able to see his face. In repose it was just as handsome as when he was awake. Cassie studied him as only an artist studies a face she wants to draw.

Suddenly he stirred and rolled toward her. She tried to move back to her side of the bed, but was trapped by an arm that flung itself across midsection. Cassie thought about trying to extricate herself, but she liked the feel of that arm around her. So she relaxed and let her head fall back against the pillow.

In no time she was asleep. And dreaming. Of the most wonderful sensations. She was gliding through the air, the sun on her face, the wind at her back. It felt so good to be touched by nature, to feel such joy, such excitement.

Only it wasn't nature creating all the delectable sensations in her. It was Mac's hand. It had worked its way beneath her satin nightshirt. She awakened with a start and discovered he was no dream. He was real. In the bed beside her. And he was awake.

And wanting her.

When he saw her eyes open, his hand stopped its journey across her flesh.

"Don't stop. It feels good," she heard her voice say, although she knew it wasn't what she was supposed to utter in the middle of the night.

They were the only words spoken between them that night as their bodies came together in the most exquisite union of love. For Cassie it was an awakening of her soul, a rebirth of the woman she thought had died four years ago.

Mac was a passionate lover, demanding she give everything, yet tender as he took her on a journey of sensory bliss. Never before had Cassie wanted a man so badly as she wanted him that night. With every beat of her heart, with every breath she took, she knew that he would forever be in her heart. And when the climax finally came, it was a joyful, tearful Cassie who trembled in ecstasy as they ended their journey.

As she fell back asleep in his arms, there was only one thought going through her mind. Their marriage was no longer make-believe.

WHEN CASSIE AWOKE the following morning she was alone in bed. She sat up and looked toward the bath, but it was dark. Sunlight peeked around the edges of the blinds and when she looked at the clock she saw that it was after ten.

Then she smiled. Was it any wonder she'd slept so late? What had happened between her and Mac last night had been very exhausting. She hugged herself at the memory, then sobered as she remembered the reason she was even in Mac's room. Tessie.

She hurried out to the kitchen and there sat her mother-in-law, reading the newspaper and listening to a talk show on the television. When she noticed Cassie, she smiled. "Good morning, dear. Sleep well?"

The twinkle in her eye had Cassie wondering if she knew just how well the night had gone. "I feel wonderful this morning," she admitted, unable to keep the smile from her face.

"I'm so glad to hear that."

"I guess Mac already left for work."

"Yes. Don't worry. I made him breakfast. He was going to cook his own because he wanted to let you sleep in, but I said that was nonsense. I know how to make my son breakfast," she said with her usual perkiness.

"That was sweet of you." Cassie didn't want to confess that the only breakfast she'd shared with Mac had been the ones they had on their honeymoon.

But that was going to change. After last night, everything was going to change, she thought as she showered in Mac's large circular stall. She'd begin tonight by making him a very special dinner. And then there'd be time for dessert....

"SMILE. IT'S FRIDAY. You've got the whole weekend off," Tabitha said to her boss that afternoon.

"Yes, I know," he said absently as he looked through the collection of medical books lining his office bookshelves.

"You and Cassie have plans for the weekend?"

At the mention of his wife's name, Mac paused to look up at his assistant. "She's finished Tessie's portrait. I suppose we'll have to take it over there."

"Sounds exciting. Well, if you don't mind, I'm going to take off early. You might want to do the same and get home to that lovely wife of yours," she said with a cheery bit of advice.

Mac didn't need any advice from anyone today—especially not when it came to Cassie. If it wasn't for the fact that he didn't want to hurt Tessie, he'd tell everyone—including the clinic staff—to stop trying to make it sound as if he had a match made in heaven. It was a marriage of convenience, for crying out loud.

Something that had been made very clear to him last night. He'd thought from the way Cassie had made love to him that she wanted it to be a real marriage, and not the sham they'd concocted for his mother's sake. She'd responded to his lovemaking with such passion, with such zest, with so much love—or what he'd thought had been love, that he was convinced they could make their marriage real. But then she'd cried. He hadn't even had the opportunity to tell her how much he loved her when the tears had poured down her cheeks. Tears for the man she still loved, the man who'd died four years ago on that very night.

He shook his head in regret. She'd warned him from the start that she wasn't in it for love. She'd even told Tessie that she'd never stop loving Darryl, that she'd buried a piece of her with him.

Now he'd tried to claim that piece. Sure she'd responded to him. She'd been half-asleep. But then when she'd realized what she'd done, how she'd betrayed the memory of her husband, she'd wept.

He was not a man to settle for another man's crumbs. If she wanted a marriage of convenience, a marriage of convenience she'd get. He wouldn't make the mistake of thinking it could be any different between the two of them.

As he finished up his paperwork, he thought about going home. Cassie wouldn't be there to cook dinner. She never was.

Tabitha was right. It was the weekend. He should have plans.

He dialed Ben Herris. "Hey, what's up?"

CASSIE COULDN'T BELIEVE Mac wasn't home. It was past eight on a Friday night. By now the dinner she'd cooked was cold, but that didn't matter. She was beginning to worry that he'd had an accident.

She contemplated what she should do. She'd tried the clinic earlier and gotten the answering service. Finally she dialed his pager, hoping he had been detained because of an emergency.

It didn't take long for her to get her answer. When the phone rang, she rushed to pick it up. "Mac?"

"Why did you page me?"

His voice was impersonal and there was a lot of noise in the background, as if he were in a restaurant or bar. "Where are you?"

"I'm having dinner with a friend. Why?"

Dinner with a friend? "Why didn't you come home?"

"Because I was hungry."

"But I thought that after last night—"

"Last night shouldn't have happened, Cassie," he interrupted her. "I'm sorry."

It shouldn't have happened? He was sorry? She couldn't believe what she was hearing.

"Look, I've got to go. It's really noisy here and I'm having trouble hearing you."

And then with a quick goodbye, he hung up.

Stunned, Cassie dropped the receiver back on the hook, then sat staring at the phone, thinking he was going to call her right back and say he'd made a mistake.

He loved her. She knew he did. How could he have made love to her like that last night if he didn't?

Then she closed her eyes. She knew the answer to that question. She'd known it all along. Because he was a player. He loved the chase, but the sweetness of the victory soon palled.

Ben Herris had unknowingly warned her at the Fourth of July picnic. Once Mac had won a woman's heart, he tired of her. Ben hadn't come right out and said so, but she knew that what he really meant was once Mac slept with a woman, the challenge was over.

He'd slept with her last night. Now he was tired of her. She was out of his system and out of his life.

Their marriage of convenience had suddenly become very inconvenient for Cassie.

CASSIE'S MINIVAN WAS NOT in the underground garage when Mac arrived home that night. That brought a frown to his face. Even though he knew it would be sweet torture to see her again after last night, the thought of not knowing her whereabouts was almost as disturbing.

According to the terms of their marriage agreement, there should have been a note on the kitchen counter telling him where she'd gone.

There was. It read, "Working at the studio." That was it. Nothing else.

So Mac went to bed alone. And he woke up alone. He didn't like either experience. It was true they'd been married less than a month, but he'd grown accustomed to her presence. She had a way of being there without being there.

When he got up and saw that Cassie hadn't come home all night, anger began to brew inside him. He knew she kept a small couch in her studio, but she'd agreed that it would be best if she slept at his place.

It didn't surprise him that last night she'd gone to the studio. It was the one place he'd never been allowed to see. He figured it was because she probably had made it a shrine to her husband, which only fueled the anger simmering inside him.

When the phone rang, it was that anger that hardened his voice.

"You certainly sound grumpy," Tessie remarked.

"I'm sorry. I didn't sleep well last night," he answered honestly.

"Is Cassie all right?"

"Why wouldn't she be?"

"When I talked to her last night she said she wasn't feeling well."

"She's fine."

"You're sure?"

"Of course I'm sure," he snapped a bit impatiently.

"Are you sure you two didn't have a little spat? It's normal, you know, for two people who love each other to disagree."

"Mom, we're fine," he stated firmly.

"That's good because I am so looking forward to the two of you coming over this afternoon with the picture."

The portrait. He and Cassie were to bring it to her today. "What time should we come?" he asked.

"Oh, anytime this afternoon."

Mac looked at his watch as he hung up the phone. He'd give Cassie until noon to call or show up.

She did neither. Shortly after noon, Mac got in his Explorer and drove over to her apartment. When nobody answered the doorbell, he let himself in with his key.

He hadn't taken two steps when Degas jumped from the back of the sofa with a meow. "Where's Cassie?" he asked the cat, who rubbed up against his legs.

"Cassie?" he called out, wondering why her minivan was in the parking lot but she was nowhere in sight.

He poked his head in each of the rooms, leaving the studio for last. He paused with his hand on the doorknob, suddenly reluctant to invade her privacy. Degas pawed at the door and meowed.

"All right, we're going in," Mac told the animal.

He pushed open the door and saw a well-lit room filled with easels and unframed canvases. But there was no artist sitting in front of any of them. Slowly Mac wandered around the room, glancing at the various pieces of art scattered about. There were no pictures of her first husband.

There was, however, a portrait of him. It was propped against an easel, a beautiful, lifelike pastel of him and Cassie, gazing at each other with adoration in their eyes. Just looking at it made the breath catch in his throat.

"What are you doing in here?"

He turned to see her standing in the doorway, a small brown sack in her hands.

"You didn't come home last night," he answered.

"I left you a note."

"Where were you just now?"

"I had to go get Degas some food. Why are you in my studio? I thought we'd agreed that you wouldn't mess with this place?" She stepped into the room and between him and the pastel on the easel.

"Where are the pictures of your husband?" he asked, giving the room a cursory glance.

"This is the only one I've done," she said, nodding over her shoulder to the pastel behind her.

"I'm not talking about me. I'm talking about Darryl."

"I never sketched him."

"Why not?"

She took a deep breath and said, "Because... because I didn't."

"You have nothing with the two of you together?"

She shook her head. "I don't want any memories of him."

"But you're still in love with him."

"No, I'm not. Why would I be in love with a man who cheated on me and left me to pay off all the bills he had from his mistress?"

"You weren't happy with him? But you said you'd never love again because of what you'd lost," he reminded her.

"Yes. I'd lost a part of me—a very trusting part that made me afraid to let my heart rule my head. But then I met you and I realized that I wanted to listen to my heart."

"And what is it saying?"

"That I've found a man who is not only a great friend, but a great lover, too," she said quietly.

He pulled her into his arms then and kissed her. "I've found the same thing. That's why I made her my wife."

"But you don't want a real wife."

He kissed her again, this time even more thoroughly and said, "If she's like the woman who was in my bed on Thursday night, I do." He pulled her tighter to him, inhaling her scent, loving the feel of her in his arms. "How could you doubt the way I feel about you after what happened that night?"

"I didn't want to, but you said you were sorry it happened?"

"Because you cried. It was the anniversary of the death of your husband. I thought that after we'd made love, you felt so awful about betraying his memory that you cried."

"But I told you that day of the wedding, I cry when I'm happy. And I was very happy that night," she said, slipping her hands inside the front of his shirt to undo the buttons.

"That was the most remarkable night of my life," he said on a sigh of pleasure as her fingers made their way down to the waist of his jeans.

"Mine, too." She continued to tease him with her exploring fingers.

"I love you, Cassie. I think I have since that night at Dinner Date," he said with his forehead resting against hers.

"I love you, too, Mac."

"I want to dissolve our marriage of convenience agreement. I want a real marriage, a real wife."

"No more pretense?"

"Just the real thing from here on out."

Epilogue

"This meeting will now come to order," Louella said with a bang of her gavel against Tessie's dining room table. "I'd like to thank Tessie for her wonderful choreography of our Christmas show. It was a huge success."

Applause accompanied the compliment and Tessie proudly stood and took a bow.

"Now as for new business," Louella said.

Tessie raised her hand and said, "Might I go first?"

"Of course. The chair recognizes Tessie."

"As you all know, I've wanted to be a grandmother for a very long time," she began.

Only Louella didn't let her finish. "Tessie, stop right there. Matchmaking we are capable of accomplishing, but babies? Not even the Mums can help Dr. Mac and Cassie with that one."

"Oh, they don't need our help," Tessie said with a grin. "You didn't let me finish, Lou. I wanted to make an announcement."

"You mean…" Louella began.

"Yes. Michael and Cassie are going to have a baby. And guess when it's due? The very day they met at Dinner Date."

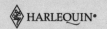

AMERICAN *Romance*

This small Wisconsin town
has some big secrets...and the
newest scandal is about to hit!

SECRET BABY SPENCER
by Jule McBride
11/00 AR #849

**PRESCRIPTION FOR
SEDUCTION**
by Darlene Scalera
2/01 AR #861

PATCHWORK FAMILY
by Judy Christenberry
12/00 AR #853

BRIDE OF DREAMS
by Linda Randall Wisdom
3/01 AR #865

And in January 2001, be sure to look for this special
3-in-1 collection from Harlequin Books!

TYLER BRIDES
by Kristine Rolofson
Heather MacAllister
Jacqueline Diamond

*Warm as a cherished family quilt and bright
as a rainbow, these stories weave together
the fabric of a community.*

Available at your favorite retail outlet.

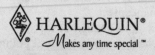

HARLEQUIN®
Makes any time special ™

Visit us at www.eHarlequin.com

HARRTT